S0-BIJ-389

PRAISE FOR

RIVER
THIEVES

"This is a splendid novel reflective of a particular place and
time. Michael Crummey is a tremendously gifted writer."
—ALISTAIR MACLEOD, author of *No Great Mischief*

"*River Thieves* is a novel of exquisite craftsmanship and
masterful artistry that should gain the broad attention it so
richly deserves: a novel of intricately balanced storytelling and
intriguing location but one also where the keen eye of a poet
resides within the language. The writing is simple and beautiful,
fully textured and gracefully rendered. Crummey has the rare
ability to breathe his characters right off the page and into the
reader's mind, where they then lodge, living on well past the
final page. *River Thieves* marks the emergence of a powerful,
mature talent." —JEFFREY LENT, author of *In the Fall*

"*River Thieves* is a novel full of poetic metaphor and memorable
images. The language and phrases of the time are richly used,
and through meticulous detail it manages to breathe life into
past ways. Most of all, it creates a vivid portrait of
Newfoundland of another era." —*The Globe and Mail*

"A little-known historical atrocity—the extinction of the Beothuk
("Red") Indians of central Newfoundland—becomes an authentic
tragedy in this brilliantly constructed, immensely moving debut
novel by an award-winning Canadian poet and short-story
writer.... There's a literary renaissance underway just north of us,
and Crummey's quite literally astonishing debut novel is one of
the brightest jewels in its crown." —*Kirkus Review*

"In the tradition of such contemporary classics as *Cold Mountain* and *In the Fall,* this beautifully written novel is both a stunning adventure story and a profound saga of courage and idealism in an imperfect world.... The last of the Beothuks died 175 years ago. But thanks to Michael Crummey, they live on in *River Thieves,* a novel of great wisdom, great power, and great heart."
— HOWARD FRANK MOSHER, author of
A Stranger in the Kingdom and North Country

"A stunningly polished and powerful book.... Crummey's craftsmanship is masterful." —*Maclean's*

"Strongly reminiscent of William Faulkner's writings ... *River Thieves* is a fascinatingly complex piece."
—*The Kingston Whig-Standard*

"*River Thieves* is a wonderful novel and Michael Crummey is a writer of enormous talent.... Michael Crummey writes like an old pro, and, not so incidently, also like an old soul, who has borne witness to tragic tendencies of humans for generations, and views them with awe and sadness and a clear-eyed compassion."
—*Ottawa Citizen*

"A rip-roaring adventure tale if ever there was one ... An exceptionally accomplished work of historical fiction that revels in the art of storytelling.... *River Thieves* is an auspicious debut for Crummey. His next novel can't come soon enough."
—*Calgary Herald*

"A haunting novel ... An engrossing and complex story that feels as authentic as a contemporary eyewitness account."
—*Elle Canada*

FLESH

AND

BLOOD

SELECTED SHORT FICTION

Michael Crummey

ANCHOR CANADA

Copyright © 1998 Michael Crummey Ink
Expanded Anchor edition 2003

All rights reserved. The use of any part of this publication, reproduced, transmitted in any form or by any means electronic, mechanical, photo-copying, recording or otherwise, or stored in a retrieval system without the prior written consent of the publisher — or, in the case of photocopying or other reprographic copying, a license from the Canadian Copyright Licensing Agency — is an infringement of the copyright law.

Anchor Canada and colophon are trademarks.

National Library of Canada Cataloguing in Publication

Crummey, Michael
    Flesh and blood / Michael Crummey.

Short stories.
ISBN 0-385-65927-X

    I. Title.

PS8555.R84F53 2002   C813´.54   C2002-903030-7
PR9199.3.C717F57 2002

Cover image: Bettmann/Corbis
Cover design: CS Richardson
Printed and bound in Canada

Published in Canada by
Anchor Canada, a division of
Random House of Canada Limited

Visit Random House of Canada Limited's website: www.randomhouse.ca

TRANS 10   9   8   7   6   5   4   3   2   1

For my brothers

CONTENTS

SERENDIPITY

When my father was assigned a home by the Company and moved out of the bunkhouse, we carried our belongings by cart and boat from Twillingate across New World Island and down to Lewisporte where we caught the train for Black Rock. Fourteen hours in the single passenger car at the end of a line of empty ore boxes and most of that time in darkness, the clatter of the rails carrying us deeper into the island's interior, into the unfamiliar shape of another life. I woke up just after first light as the train leaned into the half-mile turn of Tin Can Curve. Out the window I could see a rusty orange petticoat of abandoned scrap metal poking through the white shawl of snow at the foot of the rail bed. Twenty minutes later we crossed a trestle and chuffed into town. My father met us at the red warehouse that served as a train station, his lean face dwarfed by a fur hat, his grin lopsided, like a boat taking on water.

I'd never been away from Durrells before. Everything in this new place looked the same to my eyes. Streets as neat as garden furrows with rows of identical four unit buildings painted white or green or brown planted on either side. For the first three weeks after we arrived, my mother tied a kerchief to the door handle so my sister and I would be able to find our house in the line of uniform, indistinguishable quads.

Even my father got confused on one occasion, coming home from a card game at the bunkhouse. He'd been drinking and turned onto the street below ours, mistaking the third door in the second building for his own. Only a small lamp over the stove lighted the kitchen, the details of furniture and decoration were draped in darkness. He took off his shoes in the porch, hung his coat neatly on the wall and was about to have a seat at the kitchen table when Mrs. Neary walked in from the living room. "Can I get you a cup of tea?" she asked him.

He was too embarrassed to admit he'd made a mistake. "That would be grand, Missus," he said. "I wouldn't say no to a raisin bun if you had one to spare."

"Carl," Mrs. Neary shouted up at the ceiling. "We've got company."

For years afterwards, my father dropped in on Mr. and Mrs. Neary for tea on Saturday evenings. My father and Mr. Neary hunted together, played long raucous poker games at the kitchen table with my Uncle Gerry.

My mother said that was just like him, to find his best friend that way—everything that ever happened to my father was a happy accident. She said it with just a hint of bitterness in her voice, enough that I could taste it, like a squeeze of lemon in a glass of milk.

When I turned thirteen, my father began taking me with him to check his rabbit slips on the other side of Company property. We'd set out before dawn, following the Mucky Ditch that carried mine tailings across the bog, the squelch of footsteps in wet ground the only sound between us. When we reached the tree line we struck off for the trails through the woods. My father grinned across at me in a way that he hoped was reassuring, but

I didn't understand why he invited me along or wanted me with him. Every winter he took twice as many brace of rabbit in the slips as Mr. Neary, for no reason but chance as far as anyone could see. Of ten hands of poker, my father won eight, sometimes nine. Mr. Neary swore never to play another game on more occasions than I could count. "That man," he announced often and loudly, "has a horseshoe up his arse."

My father smiled his lop-sided grin as he shuffled the cards. "One more before you go?" he asked.

It's hard not to feel ambivalent about someone that lucky, and that casual about his good fortune. "How can you love a man," I once overheard my mother confide to Mrs. Neary, "that you never feel sorry for?"

I wouldn't have gone into the woods with my father at all if my mother hadn't encouraged me, and it was mostly for her sake that I paid attention when he showed me how to tie the slips, and how to use boughs to narrow the run where the slip was set. He explained how a night of frost set them running to keep warm. He tied the paws of the dead rabbits together with twine. "Not that lucky for these little buggers," he said lightly. I carried them over my shoulder, the bodies stiff as cordwood against my back.

Around noon we stopped to boil water for tea. "You've got a good head for the woods," my father told me one Saturday. I suppose he was trying to soften me up a little. The enthusiasm in his voice suggested he'd just discovered something I had been hiding out of modesty. "Why don't you see if you can find us a bit of dry stuff for the fire."

I tramped off into the bush, annoyed with his irrepressible good humour, with his transparent praise. He had no right, I thought, and as I moved further into the spruce I decided not to go back, to keep walking. I wanted him to panic, to feel his world coming apart as he crashed through the woods yelling my name. I wanted him to feel the sadness my mother felt, the same sick regret. I kept my head down, not bothering to check my trail, working deeper into the green maze of forest. When I stopped to catch my breath I closed my eyes, turning three times in a circle before looking up. A light snow had started falling, stray flakes filtering through the branches of the spruce like aimless stars. I had no idea where I had come from, or where I was going. I was completely, perfectly lost.

Before he moved to Black Rock, my father worked as a fisherman in Crow Head on Twillingate Island. The year he turned eighteen he courted a girl who lived with her parents down the Arm in Durrells. Every night of the week he'd walk the six miles in from Crow Head to have tea and shortbread cookies with Eliza. Then he'd walk home again, arriving after one in the morning, crawling into bed for a few brief hours before heading out on the water by six.

During the winter he walked both ways in total darkness, often in miserable weather. On a particularly blustery evening in February Eliza's family tried to convince him to spend the night, but my father politely declined. His mother was expecting him at home, and the bit of blowing snow wasn't bad enough to keep him in. The old man tapped the weather glass beside the front door. "She's dropping fast, you'd best be going if you're going."

There were no roads through Twillingate in those days. The paths quickly disappeared under snow. Wind pummelled the treeless shoreline, visibility dropped to zero. My father walked for half an hour before he decided to turn around and spend the night. An hour later he had no idea where he was. His hands and feet were numb, his eyelashes were freezing together. He hunkered below a hummock to catch his breath out of the wind. He leaned against the face of the small hill and fell backwards through the door of a root cellar. There was a bin of dark-skinned potatoes, shelves of onions, parsnip, cabbage. He was near a house. He stared through the snow looking for a sign of life in the white-out, and then marched toward what he thought might be a light in a window. My mother answered his knock at the door. "Can I get you a cup of tea?" she asked him as he unwrapped himself from his frozen winter clothes.

My grandmother went into the pantry, digging out a plateful of buns, cheese, and crackers. "Sarah," she called to my mother, "get a few blankets upstairs, we'll set him up on the daybed for tonight."

The storm went on unabated for four days. On the fifth day, my father left my mother's house to walk back to Crow Head. On the way he met his father, who had set out to look for him as soon as the weather eased up.

"Well," my grandfather said, "you're all right then."

My father grabbed both his arms through the bulk of his winter coat. "I'm getting married," he said.

My grandfather turned and they began walking back home through the thigh-deep snow. "It's about time," he said finally. "We were starting to wonder about you two."

Eliza's uncle was the merchant in Twillingate and after my parents married he made it impossible for my father to make a living as a fisherman. According to the merchant's tally at the season's end, my father's catch of salted cod didn't even cover the cost of supplies and equipment taken on credit in the spring. It was unfair and petty, but there was no recourse. My mother's oldest brother, Gerry, was working underground in Black Rock at the time and he had a word with his foreman who spoke with the Company manager. When my father left in November to start work in the mine I was already lodged in my mother's belly, undiscovered, like a pocket of ore buried in granite.

For the first eleven years of my life I saw my father only at Christmas, when he had enough time off to make the three day trip to Twillingate by train and boat. He stayed with us from Christmas Eve until Boxing Day, then began the return trip in order to be back at work on New Year's Day. I looked forward to his appearance with the same mix of anticipation and anxiety my sister reserved for Santa Claus. As if I suspected he wasn't quite real, that this year my mother would sit me down and explain he was simply a story made up for children. He arrived in the middle of the night, the pockets of his winter coat heavy with oranges and blocks of hard taffy. He sat us on his knee, our small faces disfigured by interrupted sleep and shy, helpless excitement as he bribed us with nickels to kiss the unfamiliar wool and oil smell of his cheek. Then he disappeared for another year.

As I grew older my simple disappointment with this arrangement soured. I began to suspect that he chose to live away from us, chose to visit only three days a year. It made no difference how often he explained that the Company had yet again refused his application for a house, or how lucky he was even to have a job. The promise of moving us to Black Rock was like a gift my father was constantly saving for, but could never quite afford. I had been waiting for so long that I stopped expecting it would ever happen, had stopped wanting it altogether.

Like her children, my mother became more and more accustomed to the idea of life without him. During the summers she tended the garden with my grandmother, helped her brothers cut the meadow grass for hay in the fall. She sewed and mended and knit through the winter; she taught me my sums by the light of a kerosene lamp in the evenings. For eleven years she lived alone, married to a man she knew only through occasional letters, a brief annual visit. It should have been no surprise to anyone, least of all my mother, that she was no longer in love when he finally sent for us to join him in Black Rock.

It was a Christmas tradition at the house in Durrells, before we left for Black Rock, that the story of how my parents met and became engaged would be recounted by the people present during the storm. It was an informal telling, a story thrown out piecemeal, with everyone describing their own particular role or viewpoint on this detail or that, as if they were discussing a movie they had seen together years before. My father got lost and fell backwards into the root cellar, my mother opened the door to a hill of clothes covered in snow. My mother's youngest brother caught them furtively holding hands as they sat together on the second day. Uncle Gerry slams an open palm on the table, making the glasses of whiskey and syrup jump. Nothing at all would have happened between them if he had been at home at the time, he announces, and what was my grandmother thinking to allow such a thing in the first place?

My grandmother lifts a hand from her lap-full of crochet cotton to dismiss her son's feigned outrage. "When Sarah came to my bed that night to say he'd proposed I thought, What odds about it? You lot are all alike under the clothes anyway. Go ahead and marry him if you want to, I told her. One man is as good as another."

Everyone laughs at this, my mother included. I am too young to think there could be anything prophetic in my grandmother's words.

My father says, "It was fate is what it was. It was in the stars." He digs in his pocket for a coin. "Come over my darling," he says to my mother, "and kiss me."

"You men," my grandmother says, "you're all alike."

Whatever her feelings about leaving Durrells might have been, my mother was determined to make the best of our new life in Black Rock. She thought that pretending to be a family long enough would make it real for all of us. She hoped that would be the case. She insisted we see my father off to work before each shift, turning our faces up to receive a ritual peck on the cheek. We took the Company bus out to the lake on weekends, summer and winter, sitting on a blanket on the sand or skating across to Beothuk Island. We went to matinee shows at the theatre, standing with the rest of the audience to whistle and slap the seats of our folding chairs when, inevitably, the film broke and Smitty had to splice it together before continuing. In all of these activities my mother's selfless, brittle enthusiasm was a delicate and beautiful thing, like blown glass. I travelled cautiously in the wake of that beauty, as if she was the last star in the night sky.

My sister, on the other hand, cheerfully took root. She joined the Brownie troop, the school glee club, played hop-scotch and cut-the-butter with half a dozen other children on our street. She sat in my father's arms as he played poker with Mr. Neary and my uncle, sleeping soundly through the laughter and cigarette smoke and the cursing while I sulked in my room, refusing to be placated by my mother's trays of shortbread cookies, by the second-hand pair of skates my father left on a nail in the porch. "I don't know what we're going to do with that one," my mother said whenever I retreated up the stairs.

"Don't worry," my father reassured her. "He's just miss-ing Twillingate. He'll come around. It'll all work out in the end." More than anything else, it was that blind faith in his luck that infuriated me. It hardened my resolve to show him how wrong he was about the world.

The further I walked through the bush, the more dense it became. Branches scraped my face and hands, but I hardly noticed. I was elated. I felt like shouting, but didn't want to give myself away. I kept moving, putting as much distance between myself and my father as possible, stumbling deeper into the forest like a man walking into a river, his pockets full of stones. I pictured my father scrambling through the woods behind me, calling helplessly.

Minutes later I broke through a web of alders into a clear-ing and stopped dead in my tracks. I felt something falling inside myself, a brilliant, catastrophic toppling like the collapse of a star. Twenty yards from where I stood there was a fire burning. My father crouched beside it, chewing nonchalantly on a sandwich. Lost in the bush, I realized, I had walked in a perfect circle.

"I was starting to wonder about you," my father said. "Did you find any wood for the fire?"

It was hopeless. I walked toward him, empty-handed, convinced there was no way to fight destiny, that I would never be free of my father's luck.

The following summer my mother slipped into the same posture of defeat. She abandoned her attempts to force us into the shape she thought a happy family should take, began complaining of headaches, bowing out of regular excursions and events to stay at home alone. Her absence had been so habitual and familiar to my father for so many years that he barely registered this retreat. He took my sister and I to the movie matinees without her, bought us popcorn or candies, joking with my sister as if nothing had changed. I sat sullenly through war movies and westerns starring "The Durango Kid," or a white-hatted hero played by Rocky Lane. Even during bar room brawls that hat never left his head, as if it grew from his scalp like hair. Someone in the audience inevitably shouted, "Knock his hat off!" and everyone cheered. It was enough that he always came out on top. The hat was simply flaunting it.

When we arrived home I brought my mother tea or juice where she lay in the dusk of the heavy curtains in her bedroom, her hair splayed against the pillow like meadow grass cut and drying in a field. The air in the room was thick with the smell of cloistered bodies. "You're a prince," she murmured, distracted, as if I had woken her from a dream. It was all I could do to keep from crying. Winter was coming. The stars were aligned against me.

Fate is simply chance in a joker's hat.

The Black Rock ore deposits were discovered when the stones around a prospector's cooking fire began flaring, the seams of ore in the slag bursting into flame and melting. A snow storm threw my parents together for four days and they married. My father happened on his best friend by accident. In retrospect, it can all seem inevitable, unavoidable. I think about that now, how I might have gone on hating my father forever if not for the intervention of serendipity.

Two weeks before Christmas, the Company held its annual party for employees' children at the Star Hall. My mother stayed at home, complaining of a headache. I dressed, reluctantly, while my father and sister stood in the porch, sweating under coats and scarves, shouting at me to hurry. I lagged behind them on the street, scuffing snow with the toe of my boot. My sister was in my father's arms, and they were laughing. Other families on their way to the hall congregated around them. I walked more slowly, watching as the dark cluster of people and conversation moved farther and farther ahead of me, like a train leaving a town behind. Finally I stopped altogether, angry and curiously satisfied that they hadn't noticed I was no longer beside them. I could just hear their voices at the bottom of the street and then they turned the corner.

Back at the house I pulled off my boots in the porch, feeling vaguely triumphant. My mother and I could spend the evening playing Crazy Eights, drinking tea. I knocked my boots together to clear the bottoms of snow, then set them neatly by the wall. Beside Mr. Neary's boots. I walked into the kitchen in my stocking feet. Only the light over the stove was on, there was no sound. I was about to call when I heard my mother's voice from upstairs. "Who's there?" she shouted.

"It's me," I said.

"Where's your father?" Her voice was hard, but fragile, as if the hardness in it might suddenly shatter into fragments.

"Is Mr. Neary here?" I asked uncertainly.

"Russell, you go straight to the Star Hall. Right this minute. You hear me?"

I didn't know what to say. It was like walking into a house you think is your own, taking off your shoes and jacket, sitting at the kitchen table, and suddenly realizing you're in the middle of something completely unfamiliar and unexpected, something foreign. "I forgot my scarf," I lied.

Halfway to the Star Hall I met my father, on his way back to look for me. "Well," he said. "You're all right then."

I looked at his face, at the complete innocence of it. The wind had brought tears to his eyes and he was grinning his lopsided grin at me. He had no idea. My mother and my father's best friend. For the first time in my life I felt sorry for him.

"I forgot my scarf," I lied again.

He turned toward the Hall and we walked together in the darkness. "If the wind dies down there'll be a decent frost tonight," my father said. "Tomorrow should be a good day to check the slips."

"I'd like that," I said. I reached out and held his arm through the bulk of his winter jacket. "I'd like that a lot."

AFTER IMAGE

LISE

The first time Lise saw her husband the nurses were covering his chest with petroleum jelly, the raw skin there like the eviscerated flesh of a chicken before it's cooked. His feet were black. The nurses told her they had cut off what remained of the work boots when he was brought in that afternoon and the big toes had come away with them, like pieces of charred leather.

"He was working an overhead loader near the transmission lines," Maggie Dawe explained. "Lifted the bucket right into the wires. Sixty-six thousand volts. It's a wonder he's alive at all."

She saw it in her head then, blue flames extending from his neck and shoulders like the wings of an angry angel, his face distended by the body of fire passing through him, eyes bulging in their sockets, the soles of his workboots melting on the metal floor of the loader. The sight of the man's ruined body filled her with pity and with something like desire, a feeling that she wanted to lie beside him, to feel the ghost of the voltage still coursing through his limbs. The smell of burnt hair carried from across the room, and it prickled in her nostrils like a breath of frost.

"What's his name?" she asked.

"Evans," Maggie said. "Winston Evans. From out Springdale way."

Lise smiled to herself. "He'll be fine, this one," she said. The nurses stopped and looked at her. She shrugged. "You wait and see," she said.

She told fortunes for the women in town in the evenings, after her shift at the hospital. She used cards or read the lines in the palms of their hands. She took a kerchief and burned it in a porcelain bowl, reading the ashes the same way she read tea leaves, as if the story of everything the future held already existed in the material, like genes in the body of a fetus.

Before Winston met her he had heard of people who saw auras or could heal the sick by laying their hands on the body. His grandmother once told him she'd known a seventh son of a seventh son, watched a worm held in the man's palm curl up and die in a matter of seconds, as if it was lying in a bowl of pure electrical energy.

"What's it like?" he asked Lise after they married. "What is it you see?"

Time moving through her the way fire moves through a city or a forest. Images like the negative of a photograph, darkness and light reversed. Time turned inside out.

Winston spent months recovering in hospital. Lise sat with him on her breaks, lighting his cigarettes, holding them to his mouth so he could inhale. When he had healed enough to be washed, she talked the nurses into letting her bathe him twice a week in his bed, barely touching him with a wet cloth. Her hands tingled, as if his body was still charged and giving off small electric shocks. She lifted him forward to wash his back, brushing gently down the ribbed line of his spine, a mark black as an eel scorched along the length of it by the passage of the electric current. She squeezed water over the curl of his penis in its singed patch of pubic hair, its small blue head resting helplessly on a thigh. She looked up at his face to see him watching her, without hope or fear, and she leaned across the bed to take him into her mouth, holding him there so he could feel her warmth. She stared up at him again, his eyes closed, his expression slack with patient resignation. His helplessness was complete, but temporary, it hummed with the promise of vigour and energy. And that promise made his impotence seem dumbly affectionate to Lise, as if he was a family dog lying still while a toddler harmlessly tormented him. She straightened and stroked the soft flesh with her cloth, then moved down his legs toward the feet.

"Don't worry," she told him, smiling, "it'll come back to you."

She already knew they would marry. There would be children. He fell in love with her confidence, with her hands on his body in places he had never been touched by a woman before.

LEO

Leo was the middle child. Quiet and withdrawn, he lived on the fringe of the family like a victim of leprosy living on the outskirts of a city in the Bible. His sister and brother had their mother's copper-coloured hair and pale freckled skin. They were ambidextrous. He sported a head of ordinary mousey-brown locks and a ruddy, dark complexion. And although he practised when no one was around, he couldn't teach himself to properly hold a fork or a pencil with his left hand.

Theresa and Jerome had also inherited something else from their mother, something both more and less obvious than the colour of their hair. They were strange, peculiar in a way that made people—Leo included—uneasy. There was a disorienting calm about them. Like their mother burning kerchiefs in the living room, staring at the ashes with the serenity of a student holding cheat notes, predicting money, marriage, a death in the family.

At school Leo's brother and sister were looked upon in the same way children look at a dead animal, with a mixture of awe and distaste. In the line-up at the canteen during recess, the students standing closest to Theresa and Jerome were careful not to come into physical contact with them. If a hand brushed an arm, even their clothes, a whisper snaked through the line: "So and so has the Evans Touch." The only way to rid yourself of the stigma was to pass it on to someone else. The Evans Touch moved through the school yard like a spark of static electricity passed from hand to hand. Sometimes a child would approach Leo from behind, tagging his arm or the back of his neck, shouting, "You've got the Evans Touch!" It was the mousey-brown hair that fooled them. It wasn't until he turned around that they realized who he was.

He found a red baseball cap and wore it constantly, taking it off only when he was ordered to, in school or at the table during meals. He wanted to shave his head or dye his hair some outrageous colour, purple or green, but he had no idea how to go about it. He got into fights in the school yard when he overheard boys passing the Evans Touch.

Theresa wiped the blood from his nose and mouth with a tissue afterwards. "You can't change things like this," she told him.

It made him feel like crying to hear her talk that way. It was as if she could read the future and saw the futility of any attempt to alter himself or the world. It made him feel like hitting her too, like pulling her copper-coloured hair from her head.

Leo often fantasized about leaving, about hitch-hiking out of town and never coming back. Lise looked at him sadly, as if she could tell what he was thinking. "Is your life so terrible?" she asked him, her palms cupping his face.

He pushed away from her, from the warmth of her hands on his skin. It was all her fault, he was sure of it. Theresa and Jerome had been indelibly marked by his mother. Even his father carried scars that set him apart from everyone else in town: parts of his face looked permanently and painfully sunburned, almost purple, his hair was as fine and wispy as an infant's. Leo had no evidence beyond intuition, but he was convinced that his father's appearance was somehow connected to his mother as well.

Leo spent as much time alone in the house as he could, crawling into cupboards or the cubbyhole in the basement. He sat in complete silence, not moving, comforted by the darkness. He thought if he practised long enough he might be able to disappear altogether. Sometimes he was missing for hours, but his mother never seemed to worry about him, never made any attempt to root him out or change his behaviour. She walked through the house at night turning out the lights on her way to bed. "Goodnight, Leo," she said aloud, as if she knew he was somewhere within her hearing.

When Leo was eleven, a travelling photographer came through town, going door to door with the latest in photographic technology, offering to take portraits *in colour*. He sat the Evans family on the chesterfield in their living room, arranging hands and the tilt of their heads, standing back to study the effect of the whole. He moved Leo to his mother's lap, sat him between his brother and sister, then at the end of the chesterfield, as if the boy was a piece of a jigsaw puzzle that didn't fit. Finally he put Leo on the floor in front of the group.

"That's it," he said, his head hidden behind the camera. "Everybody smile." The flash was so bright they saw stars before their eyes.

The picture was framed and placed on an end-table in the living room. Leo's face sullen, stoic, as if he was convinced the camera was about to steal his soul.

WINSTON

Winston grew up in a house with his parents and his grandmother on the east coast of the island. One autumn night a thunderstorm rolled in off the ocean, each room of the house perfectly illuminated by an almost constant strobe of lightning, the family a frozen tableau where they were gathered around the wood stove. There was a kerosene lamp on the table, its small flame shaken by thunder.

His grandmother got up to add a junk of wood to the fire, her movement across the room stuttered into slow motion by the rapid flash of light. As she opened the stove door lightning entered the house through the chimney, a ball of white fire tinged with purple shooting past the old woman's bent figure and into the kitchen. It circled the base of the walls around them, like an animal stalking its prey. The entire episode took place in a matter of seconds, although in Winston's mind the speed and strangeness of the event filled those moments with an almost infinite panic: he sat frozen to his chair, watching his grandmother pick up her broom, walk calmly to the kitchen door and sweep the lightning outside. The after image of brightness was a circle of darkness on their retinas for fifteen minutes afterwards.

He told his children this story during another storm, years later. The power was out and they had gathered in the darkness of the living room, the glow of a single candle on the coffee table. "Stare at the candle," Winston told them, "then close your eyes." Theresa and Jerome tapped each others' shoulders blindly. "I can see it," they shouted. "I can see it."

Leo didn't believe a word of his father's ridiculous story and refused to stare at the candle with his brother and sister. Their shared enthusiasm made him feel deliberately excluded and he wandered off to hide somewhere else in the house, to be away from them all. Winston looked across at Lise and she shrugged helplessly. For a long time now he thought they should tell Leo, but Lise refused.

"Whether we say anything or not, he knows," Winston argued. "He can tell he doesn't belong."

"It's just a phase," Lise told him. "He'll get over it."

Winston shook his head. "You call yourself a fortune teller," he said.

After his accident in the loader, Winston lost his sight for several weeks. The doctor told him the damage to his eyes could be permanent and he might never see again. Lise sat beside him, holding cigarettes to his lips, telling him different. By then he knew she worked in the kitchen and laundry, that she wasn't even a nurse.

"What do you look like?" he asked her.

"Like a witch," she said. "Red hair. Green eyes. I'm left-handed as well as right-handed. I was born on Friday the 13th."

He didn't believe a word of it. "Are you trying to frighten me off?" he asked.

He could tell when she entered and left the room, felt her presence and absence, as if he and Lise were opposite ends of a magnet. When his sight returned he could see only in shades of grey for the first few days. The image of Lise beside him blurred, indistinct. "Your hair," he said, looking into her face for the first time. "What colour is it?"

LISE

A month after Theresa was born, Leo's mother came to see her. She had arrived in Black Rock several months before and worked as a housekeeper at the Staff House. She was just eighteen, mousey-brown hair tied back with a barrette, her red face bunched like a fist. They sat together in the living room and Lise watched her for a moment before speaking. "You're pregnant," she said finally.

The woman brought a hand to her mouth and held it there.

"You have questions about the father?"

"No." She cleared her throat. "No, I know the answers to those questions already. So, I want to know what will happen. What will become of me and the baby."

Lise nodded. "Give me your kerchief."

She held the cloth over the porcelain bowl, the flames travelling upward toward her hand, then she dropped it and let it burn itself out. She lifted the bowl into her lap and stared.

The woman leaned toward her, trying to peer in herself. "Well?" she said.

Lise looked up at her without speaking.

"What is it?" the woman said.

She was working a four to twelve shift when Leo's mother arrived at the hospital months afterward, already in labour. Two hours later Maggie Dawe was on the phone trying to locate the doctor. "There are complications," she explained. "Tell him to get here as soon as he can." Lise sat in the laundry room, hiding in the noise of the machines sloshing loads of bedding and uniforms, waiting for it to be over.

The baby was bundled and sleeping in the nursery the first time she laid eyes on him. He had a purple mark on his forehead shaped like a candle flame that would fade within a week, although Lise couldn't predict this from looking at him. In fact, she saw nothing, could tell nothing about the boy, good or bad.

As she stood watching him, Leo woke and began crying. She felt the weight of the milk in her breasts. It had been hours since she nursed Theresa and the front of her uniform was suddenly wet. She stepped forward and lifted him from his crib, sitting with him in her lap, unbuttoning quickly, holding her nipple to the tiny mouth, her pale skin against his angry red face.

She was still nursing him when Maggie Dawe entered the room. "We can take him," Lise said, looking up from the baby. "Me and Winston. I knew the girl a little, it only makes sense."

Maggie stared at them for a moment. "I'll speak to the doctor," she said.

LEO

When the cubbyhole in the basement became too cold in the winter, Leo hid in his parents' closet. He sat listening to the movements of his family outside the closed door: his brother and sister brushing their teeth in the bathroom, the toilet flushing; the kettle whistling downstairs; the front door opening and closing as his father left to work the night shift at the mill, the squeak of his boots on the surface of the snow outside. He fell asleep before his mother walked through the house, turning out the lights.

Her footsteps outside the closet door woke him. A wedge of light fell across his face as she reached in to pull out a nightdress. From where he sat against the wall Leo watched his mother remove her skirt and blouse, and pull her hair band free of the long copper ponytail. He could see the constellation of beauty marks across her shoulders. He wanted to turn away, to shut his eyes or shout something, but he sat there without moving, without uttering a sound. She unhooked her bra, letting it fall from her shoulders and Leo stared at her breasts, the pale weight of them below an elaborate necklace of freckles, the large brown nipples erect in the chill air of the house.

He couldn't recall ever seeing his mother's breasts before, but he remembered nursing at them, the smell of her skin and her face leaning above him, her voice speaking his name. He didn't understand why there was no visible sign to mark him as hers, why he alone had been passed over. He thought of the warmth of her milk in his mouth and felt a surge of loneliness that emptied him like an overturned bottle. It was as if he had finally succeeded, as if he had disappeared completely and only his absence would go on inhabiting the house from that moment forward.

He waited in the darkness for a long time after the light was put out, until he was sure his mother was asleep. Downstairs he lifted the family portrait from the end table in the living room, picked up his mother's porcelain bowl and carried both to the basement. The lighter fluid was packed away with half a bag of barbecue coals. He removed the picture from its frame, placed it in the porcelain bowl between his legs, and soaked it with the clear liquid. He shook the tin until it was empty. He took a match and struck it against the box, holding the small flame in the air a moment, then dropping it into the pool of lighter fluid just inches beneath his face.

WINSTON

It was the only moment of prescience Winston had ever experienced. Just before three in the morning, coming up on break. He was raking through a floatation tank at the ore mill, his reflection moving beneath him in the metallic green and silver liquid. The image rose up and washed over him, passing through his entire body like an electric current. The brilliant flash, the sound of the boy's cry. When he closed his eyes he could see the after image of the fire moving against the darkness.

"Leo," he said aloud.

He spent days beside the boy's hospital bed, watching the small body: the rise and fall of the chest, the bandaged face and head. The cotton patches over the eyes.

"Will he be able to see?" he whispered to Lise.

She shrugged and looked at her hands in her lap. "I think he will," she said. "I can't say for sure."

Winston reached across to take her hand. It had frightened them both, her inability to know what might happen to the boy, the fact that she hadn't foreseen the accident. As if he was a permanent blind spot in her range of vision.

"The little arsehole," Lise murmured, furious with Leo suddenly, as if he had been hiding these things from her deliberately. "Once he gets out of that bed I'll teach him to play with matches."

"It's just a phase," Winston said, trying to smile across at his wife. "He'll get over it."

The day the bandages came off Leo's eyes, Winston and Lise were there with him. The curtains were drawn at the windows and the overhead lights were turned out. The doctor warned him not to open his eyes right away. His lids flickered like a candle flame guttering in a breeze. Tears rolled down his cheeks.

After a few minutes the doctor turned on a shaded lamp in the corner and Leo closed his eyes against the sudden brightness.

"What is it?" Winston asked.

"I can see it," Leo said, his eyelids still shut tight. "I can see it."

Winston looked across at his wife. She was staring at Leo's face and smiling, studying the scars as if they were a map of the future. "Yes," she said quietly, like she had expected this all along. "Yes you can."

After Leo got out of hospital Winston often caught him looking at himself in the mirror, studying the scars on his face, the fluff of hair on his head slowly growing back in, the smooth reptilian look of the lashless eyelids. For a while Winston had thought it might be better for him not to regain his sight at all.

He was afraid for him, worried he would never adjust to the change in himself, the disfigurement. But that wasn't what Winston saw in the boy now. It was as if Leo was recovering from amnesia and just beginning to recognize his own face in the mirror. There was a look of wonder in his eyes. And something more tangible than that, Winston thought.

Confirmation.

HEARTBURN

andy Wilcox is dreaming.

Prickle of sharp air in his lungs. His feet are numb with the cold and wet, the salt water soaking through his boots, his two pair of wool socks, the thick pads of the heels where they've been darned. The sparse horseshoe of two storey houses in North Harbour is splayed behind him, the white puzzle of the ice field stretches to the horizon. He is copying from one pan to another, each stepping stone of ice dipping below the freezing water as it takes his weight, surfacing again as he moves quickly onto the next.

He can hear voices all around him, the shouts of other boys on the ice pans, although there is no one else nearby that he can see and he has the peculiar sensation of being completely alone. He is moving away from the shoreline, the exhilaration of the first minutes on the ice giving way now to fatigue and panic, the size of the pans diminishing as he moves, each one sinking a little deeper than the last, his pants soaked through to the knee. He knows the ice won't hold his stationary weight, that if he stops he'll fall through. His lungs feel raw, as if they've been flayed by a knife, he can taste blood in his mouth. Before long he knows he will fall, exhausted, that he'll sink into black water, dragged down by the weight of his soaked clothing, and he runs awkwardly over the sloppy ice to save his life.

He surfaces in darkness. The initial relief of escaping the dream lasts only moments. His eyes are open but the black is close, impermeable, as snug as a blindfold. His body is soaked in sweat, his head aching from dehydration and the heat of the earth this far underground and the lingering stink of blasting powder. They have been under more than forty-eight hours now, just the one headlamp between them still has juice and they use it only when necessary.

He is lying back against bare rock. It hurts to breathe and he feels as if he is slowly drowning, the remaining oxygen in the drift being wrung from the air like water from a towel. He can hear the other men breathing around him like the sound of animals snuffling outside a canvas tent. He tries desperately to recall their names and faces. There are five of them, but that's all he can bring to mind, the number, and it terrifies him to think they may have forgotten him in the same way.

By this point he recognizes that he is still dreaming, recognizes the dream, although there is no comfort in the recognition of these things, and he begins to will himself awake by shouting. If he screams loud enough it will carry up through the overburden of sleep and drag him back with it.

Georgie is asleep beside him.

He lies still, reaching a hand to brush against the warmth of her skin through the nightdress. The window is open and he can hear the sound of wind in the trees outside. It could be he is still dreaming. Even the peace of this domestic scene could go wrong suddenly, close in on him. His heart is racing and he breathes deeply to calm himself, taking in the cool air coming through the window. It's a good sign. He can never breathe properly in the dreams. After a few moments he lifts his legs carefully over the side of the bed so as not to disturb Georgie and gets up.

He pads quietly out of the room and downstairs. No sense trying to sleep for a while. It's a queer thing, sometimes he wakes himself four or five times, only to discover he has surfaced into another nightmare, as if he's trying to escape a building on an elevator and continually getting off at the wrong floor. He takes the milk from the refrigerator, pours a glass and carries it into the living room. He considers sitting in the recliner and decides against it; too comfortable, he might drift off again. Instead he sits in Georgie's knitting chair, the broken spring in the seat digging into his backside. He's been promising to fix it for years, but is glad now for the persistent node of discomfort that will help keep him awake, alert.

And then Georgie appears in the doorway to the hall, her arms folded across her chest, her feet bare. Her grey hair and her nightshirt are ghostly white in the glow of the streetlight outside. "Bad night?" she asks, gravel in her voice.

He shrugs, holds up the glass of milk as if he's about to offer a toast. "Heartburn," he says. He hasn't told her about the dreams and doesn't intend to. She'll think he's going off his head. "You go on to bed," he tells her. "I'll be up in a bit."

When she turns away, he stops her. "Georgie?"

Her hand is still on the frame of the doorway, her face looking at him over her shoulder.

"No, nothing," he says. "Nevermind. I'll be up in a bit."

She supposes she might never have married Sandy if he hadn't gone through the ice that winter and drowned.

Her mother used to say he was destined for it, what with the way his eyebrows grew together like that, an unbroken hedge of thick blonde hair across his forehead. "No way his mother should let that boy out in a boat," she said. Georgie had never looked at him as anything other than shy Sandy Wilcox before she heard her mother speak of him that way. He was plain looking, no question, and the single eyebrow made him appear less intelligent than he deserved to be given credit for. The pity she felt for him was an ordinary, uncomplicated thing before she learned it was a portent of something more mysterious and severe.

She wondered if he could tell, if he had a knowing inside to match the external mark of his fate. It would be an awful thing, she thought, to grow up with that awareness lodged inside you like a tumour. If he did, he gave no indication, and Georgie took his reticence as a sign of stoicism, of uncommon courage in the face of looming, inevitable disaster. It made him seem tragic and beautiful in her eyes and at the time there was nothing more she needed to fall in love.

As it happened, she was along the shore when he went through the ice that year. March of 1952. None of the other boys could reach him, the pans not large enough to hold their weight. They had to run for his father and then launch a skiff into the slobby ice, half poling, half hauling toward the spot where he'd last been seen, the rescuers going through to their waists and hauling themselves up by the gunnell, using the oars to pole to more solid ice and going over the side to pull further along. It was fifteen or twenty minutes at least before they reached him and dragged the body out from under the ice like a dead seal. A cold crescent of water sprayed from his sleeves as he flopped over the side into the boat.

She followed the group carrying the body back to the house. Sandy's father, Ned, held Sandy under the armpits, the boy's face against his chest bleached white by the water, his lips as dark as bilberries. Ned had a walrus mustache and a red, pinched face that made him look permanently angry. "Look out now," he shouted whenever Jeb Walsh, who had one of Sandy's feet, stumbled on the rocky path. "Hold him *up*, would you," he said.

At the house, the entire procession trooped through the door and into the kitchen where Sandy was laid out on the table. Martha Wilcox had seen them heading up from the harbour and was already wailing when they came in. There were twelve or thirteen people crowded into the tiny room where Martha had been baking bread and the heat was overwhelming. Georgie had never seen a dead person before and she was afraid she might be sick to her stomach.

Ned Wilcox tried to hold his wife, but she pushed him off and leaned over her son, crying helplessly. "Now woman," Ned said, "there's no bloody help in that." She ignored him and went on weeping. She clutched at the boy's clothing and shook him and finally punched on his chest with her rough fists. "Martha!" Ned shouted. "Jesus," he said. But Jeb Walsh held him back by the arm and he finally turned away from the spectacle of his keening wife striking their dead son.

No one else uttered a word. Georgie can remember the lonely sound of the woman's fists on Sandy's chest like someone beating a rug. And then Sandy convulsed on the table, spat up a mouthful of water and started into a fit of coughing. His mother put both her hands to her head and screamed. And Georgie fainted dead away on the floor.

"She swooned," is how Sandy likes to describe it. "Only time I've ever swept a woman off her feet."

"I was fifteen," Georgie says flatly. "And you scared the bejesus out of me. Some romance."

There was a time, Sandy remembers, when she went along with him. When she'd hold the back of her hand to her forehead, flutter her eyelids as if she was reliving that moment. "Handsome?" she'd say. "My God, you looked better laid out dead than you ever have alive." Laughter from the company assembled, friends up to the house for a drink, or sitting around the table at a Legion dance. He tries to remember when their easy way with it changed, but supposes it could have gone on for years before he noticed the difference.

Stan and Laura Caines get up to take a turn on the dance floor, Everett King heads to the bar for a round of drinks. Georgie watches after Everett, his peculiarly stiff walk a memento of the accident in the mine. "He's doing alright since losing Sylvia," she says. "I thought he'd shrivel up and die."

Sandy looks down into his glass. "I s'pose you'd do alright without me too," he says. "If you had to."

He's gotten so maudlin these days. Hardly sleeping at night, sitting up with old photo albums of the wedding, the children when they were youngsters. And this kind of foolishness. Now's a fine time, she thinks, to be getting sentimental, to fall in love with a wife. "You're not planning on running off with some young thing are you Sandy?"

He laughs. "You've seen my ankles," he says. "I won't be running anywhere anytime soon."

Everett comes back with his fists crowded with glasses. He sits them on the tabletop and slides them like chess pieces to the circle of chairs. Sandy lifts his drink and swallows a good mouthful.

"Yes now laddy-buck," Georgie says to him. "You'll be up all night again if you keep at the whiskey like that."

Everett raises his glass to Sandy. "Nevermind the old battleaxe," he says. "We can't afford to waste the few hours left to us asleep anyways."

Sandy reaches into the pocket of his suit coat and pulls out a roll of Tums. "I came prepared," he says.

He's been dreaming about the child. The one they lost, their first.

In the dream the child is inside his body, not Georgie's. There is no change in him that he can tell, no outward sign, but he senses the baby's presence, how his flesh surrounds it. His lungs feel crowded and inefficient; he can barely catch his breath. And he can feel the baby's urge to be clear of him, its panic, as if it was buried underground already. He strips off his clothing and examines himself, looking for an escape route for the child. Ridiculous, it gives him the shivers to remember this part of the dream, searching his own body for an opening that doesn't exist.

And then the dream changes. The child changes in the dream, and suddenly there is a dead thing inside him. How did Georgie bear it? He wants it out of him; he never wants it to leave his body. In the dream he begins bawling helplessly, a grief unlike anything he's ever felt coming over him, his body shaking, convulsing. And it's the weeping that wakes him.

He's afraid that one of these nights he'll cry out in his sleep, that he'll sob loud enough to wake Georgie. He lies beside her stillness, snuffling as quietly as he can, wiping his eyes with the hairy backs of his hands. He wishes he'd been less gruff with her at the time, less sensible about the whole thing.

He came to the hospital as soon as word reached him underground and stood in the doorway to Georgie's room, feeling awkward in his work clothes, his face still black with rock dust. More than anything he was embarrassed by the whole affair, as if he'd unexpectedly fallen in front of a crowd of spectators. The best that could be done in such a situation, he felt, was to carry on as if nothing had happened. He walked over to his wife and held her hand while she cried quietly in her bed. "Now woman," he said. "There's no help in that. We'll have others."

She had fixed him then, as if she'd just recognized him for someone she disliked and might someday learn to despise. "We're not collecting a set of dishes," she said. "It was a *baby* Sandy."

It's a wonder, he thinks now, that Georgie stuck it out with him for so long.

Georgie can still recall the night she made up her mind to leave her husband.

She had gone to bed before Sandy and was nearly asleep when he made his way quietly up the stairs to the bedroom. He undressed in the darkness, not wanting to disturb her with the light, then settled in beside her, his hands moving firmly across her back. She rolled over and pushed her face into his chest, automatically reaching under her nightshirt to help him fumble off her underwear, then turning to lie beneath him. He kissed the side of her face once, twice, and then lay still.

It was after he fell asleep that she started, almost sat bolt upright in bed. In the darkness she couldn't picture his face. Her heart hammered against her chest. Seventeen years of marriage, three children, and she had suddenly forgotten what the man looked like.

The thought that he might sometimes forget her in the same way made her skin crawl. She thought of him moving over her in the darkness without uttering a sound, and it struck her then that she had never heard him say the word love in her presence. His father's son, after all. Practical to a fault, plain-spoken. Plain-looking too, though she couldn't bring the details together to see his face in her head just at that moment. She slipped out of bed, heading downstairs where she sat in his recliner until the first grey light of dawn lifted the room out of darkness. She considered how long things had been the way they were, how numb she had become, as if she had spent a decade submerged in frigid water. Made up her mind.

The following night, Sandy started on midnights. She did up his lunch tin, made him a cup of tea, saw him through the door. Then she went upstairs to pack, allowing herself one suitcase for her things, one for the kids. She wrote Sandy a letter, telling him she would be staying with her mother in North Harbour, that he could come and take the car whenever he wanted it.

She woke the children at six. Helen, who was almost twelve, helped her dress the two boys. "It's a surprise," was Georgie's answer to every question about why they were up so early, and why the suitcases were packed, and where they were going without Daddy. She sat them at the table with bowls of cereal and carried the suitcases out to the car. She looked up at the sky, the long surf of pink light at the horizon beyond the row of houses as bright as a fresh scar. At that moment there was a waver in her heart, a doubt. And that's when the Company siren began wailing.

After the local news Georgie lifts herself up out of the knitting chair and sets two pairs of wool socks with newly darned heels on the seat. Sandy watches her as she walks into the kitchen for a last glass of water before bed. There's a slight limp in her step and he feels a momentary pang of guilt about the broken spring in her chair. He could fix the damn thing, but he's afraid Georgie will read into it, that she'll think he's getting soft in his old age. He isn't about to let on if he can help it.

"You coming?" Georgie asks from the foot of the stairs.

"You go ahead. I'll be up in a bit."

Sandy has taken to staying awake as long as he can these days, partly because the dreams have become more persistant, and partly because it's a chance to leaf through the family photos in the cabinet under the coffee table without Georgie knowing. He hadn't paid much attention when she spent hours painstakingly putting the albums together, and couldn't see the sense in it when she wrote names and dates on tiny scraps of paper and taped the captions below each picture. "If you're that bored," he had said. "I wish you'd put as much effort into making a bit of supper," he had told her. "Would you lift your head out of those goddamn pictures for two minutes?" he'd said.

There is one page in particular that he finds his way back to every time he sits with the stack of albums in his lap. Like an alcoholic lured by the gravitational pull of a bar, Sandy inches towards a photo of a tiny grave marked by a white wooden cross. *Andrew Samuel Wilcox* in Georgie's careful handwriting. At the time, Sandy saw no point in naming the child and agreed to it only at Georgie's furious insistence. But he can't imagine anything quite as distressing as the thought of looking at this photo now without a name in his head to connect to it. He's wanted to tell Georgie this for months, but has never found the words or the courage.

It sometimes seems to Sandy as if he's lived all his days on that ice field in his dream, running to save his life and not looking back. As if he's slipped through his sixty odd years without paying enough attention to the world to remember the order of the seasons. For reasons he doesn't understand, he is just now becoming aquainted with himself, and he spends hours with the pictures, trying to set their peculiarly layered chronology to memory. As if they might be able to return a life he long ago misplaced.

Everett King is over for his daily snort. Ever since his Sylvia passed on he's made a habit of dropping by around three in the afternoon for a whiskey or two. It breaks up the day, he says, makes the house feel that much less lonely.

Georgie keeps a close eye on them. Occasionally she's slipped and they've gone and gotten themselves drunk before supper and then the silly buggers get out of hand. Reminiscing. Going back underground. Reliving the accident. Everett's leg was badly mangled by the rock fall and he spent the three days slipping in and out of consciousness. For his part, Sandy claims to have spent the whole time praying to see his three darling children again, to lie one more time in the arms of his wife. "Drunken old fool," is what Georgie thinks when he gets on like that. He has never said a word to that effect when he's sober.

"Georgie," Everett says, "you were a saint to my Sylvia. You were a rock, you were." There's a tell-tale quiver in his voice. "She always said she'd have gone right off her head if you hadn't been there with her."

"Now Ev," she says sternly, "don't you go getting teary here this afternoon. I won't have it, you hear me? And that's your last drink for today, I can tell you that. You too," she says to her husband as she gets up to start supper in the kitchen.

"Saint Georgina!" Sandy toasts, his almost empty glass in the air, and Everett offers a hearty "Hear, hear."

"Oh fuck off, the both of you," Georgie mutters.

It comes out angrier than she means it. And it's mostly guilt, she knows. Guilt about the fact that she *was* a rock through the whole ordeal. She spent her time comforting and encouraging the families of the other men underground with her husband. She fed and cared for her kids, for Sylvia's and for Laura Caines's four boys on top of that. She's ashamed to admit to herself that, more than anything, she was angry with Sandy. The thought never once crossed her mind that he might die, that she might lose him for good. There were moments when she was convinced this latest catastrophe was simply an elaborate attempt to hold onto her. As if he had planned it to happen just as she was about to leave him.

It wasn't until he arrived home safe and sound that she felt any pity for him at all. There were weeks of him waking from the same nightmare of being lost underground, crying out in the darkness. She'd *shush* him gently and hold him for hours afterwards, rocking him in her arms. It seemed impossible to her then, the thought of him waking up alone in this house, without her or the children. And almost despite herself, the pity worked at whatever was left of her love for him, the way ashes are stirred to build a new fire. It was a slow spotty fire by and large, the dirty bit of smoulder you get from burning green wood, more smoke and irritation than warmth. But enough finally to keep her where she was, and where she is now: mixing weaker and weaker drinks for an old man in the afternoon; clipping his thick yellow toenails once a month; allowing him the pleasure of an occasional waltz at the Legion. She'd made up her mind to stop being unhappy a long time ago.

"Georgie," her husband calls from the living room. "Any chance of one more little one for Ev before he heads home?"

He dreams of his panic beneath the ice when he was a boy, his exhausted body pressed to the cold weight of it above him; blur of blue-green light on his face like the colour cast by stained glass, an opaque barricade between himself and his life.

Then there is the heat of the kitchen and the sound of a woman crying, his body being roughly shaken; the thumping on his chest, as if someone was knocking at a door to wake a sleeper in a distant part of the house.

When Georgie finally manages to shake him awake his face is wet with tears.

"Sandy," she's saying, "Sandy, wake up."

He looks at the face leaning over his own as if it's the face of a stranger, a person he knew years ago and can't quite place. "What a Christly racket you were making," Georgie says, wiping the tears from his cheeks with the palm of her hand. His expression is silent and imploring, edged with equal parts desperation and embarrassment, like the face of a man who has been paralyzed by a stroke. The dream hasn't begun to leave him yet and the features of the room and the woman beside him have a slightly other-worldly feel, the grey of dawn nuzzling the windows, the edges of things softened by the dim light.

"What was it," his wife asks him. "What were you dreaming about?"

He shakes his head, the tears coming again, his body wracked with sobs. His lungs feel waterlogged, useless. There's a burning sensation in his chest, it hurts simply to breathe. He buries his face in Georgie's chest and holds onto the warmth of her body. Prays he will never wake up.

ROOTS

AN ACT OF GOD

Ian's father dies in church, half way through the sermon.

The minister's words have begun to string out in languorous, folding arcs like strands of pulled taffy. His father hears the Pharisees and Judas, he hears what might be *thirty pieces of silver* and then it seems he is listening to a nest of bees in the rafters. He tries to discreetly signal his wife in the choir loft, raising a finger in front of his chest, then collapses forward and sideways onto the floor.

His mother hears the gurgle in his throat and a muffled thump, thinks to herself *Someone is gone*. When she half-rises from her seat to pinpoint the source of the noise, her husband is out of view, buried under the stained wood of the pews. A dark hedge of parishioners has circled the fallen man by the time she reaches him. She pushes through, grips the fabric of her husband's suit coat and pulls him free into the aisle. "I can't find a pulse," she says aloud, three fingers pressed into the loose skin of his neck. A woman standing behind her is whispering "Please, God. Please, God."

"No," his mother says. "Nothing." She removes the neck tie, raises a fist and thumps his chest, the slap of flesh and bone muffled by the fabric of the white Sunday-best shirt. A gasp of air leaves his father's mouth, his eyes flutter briefly. Then nothing. She raises her fist again, strikes, her glasses slumping forward on her nose, her bra strap falling from her right shoulder. The dull thump. A sharp intake of breath like a rush of water breaking through a clogged drain. His father's eyes opening wide, like a new-born's, disoriented, mildly surprised. She turns his head to the side as he vomits, and the minister comes running from the vestibule to announce the ambulance is on its way. *He was dead*, Ian's mother is thinking. *He was dead*. And as he slowly comes to his senses, his father is thinking exactly the same thing.

A DISCOVERY, ITS CONSEQUENCES

Near Beothuk Lake in central Newfoundland, the island's granite rock is veined with ore. Thick cables of raw mineral snake for miles beneath the landscape of bog and shrub land, like threads of coloured wool sewn haphazardly into a black sweater.

The first evidence of these was discovered early in the century by Cary Mullen, the son of a Mi'kmaq woman and an Irishman from the tiny seaside town of Black Rock. Mullen was employed by the Anglo Newfoundland Development Company to look for sulphur deposits to be used in the pulp and paper operations at Grand Falls. As he settled in at a campsite after several weeks of fruitless prospecting, Mullen noticed that pieces of rock near his cooking fire were flaring, breaking into flame, and melting. He scorched his hands in the rush to pull the burning rocks away from the fire and he immediately shipped them to Grand Falls where assay tests revealed a high concentration of lead, zinc, and copper, with traces of gold and silver.

For the rights to his find, Mullen was paid two dollars and fifty cents—the equivalent of a bag of flour. Subsequent trenching and exploratory shafts sunk by the American Smelting and Mining Company of New York revealed several deposits of ore, the richest running as high as forty-one percent combined zinc, lead and copper. Underground work began in 1907, but due to the exorbitant cost of separating the ore the mine was closed in 1909. It wasn't until the early 1920s that a floatation technology capable of turning the Black Rock finds into a profitable operation was developed.

In 1925, a second round of prospecting and mining began under the direction of Philip J. Ward. A vertical shaft was sunk across the Black Rock River, opposite the 1907 site, in hopes of locating a faulted eastward extension of the ore, but a heavy overburden and difficult spring run-off conditions hampered the work and it was quickly abandoned. At the same time, Hans Nordlund, a pioneer of electrical geophysical prospecting, was surveying land within a square mile radius of the original shaft. On July 14th, 1926, Nordlund was working in a section of wet and boggy land three hundred feet east of the original shaft when he discovered one of the largest bodies of ore uncovered in North America. Two to three feet beneath the bog, the bedrock revealed massive mineralization. Work crews and diamond drill rigs were immediately moved to the site. One hundred and four feet below the surface, the rig drilled through seven feet of ore. The drill was moved one hundred feet to the north and angled to intersect the vein one hundred feet deeper. On August 7th, this hole drilled into fifty-five feet of ore.

Ward immediately telegraphed New York.

STRIPPING STRONG LEAD ZINC ORE BODY FIVE
HUNDRED FEET EAST OF ORIGINAL SHAFT   STOP
INDICATIONS POINT TO IT BEING LARGER THAN
MAIN MINE   STOP   CONGLOMERATE SHAFT
CROSSCUT VEIN TEN FEET WIDE CROSSCUT
NORTH INTO FIFTY-FIVE FEET   STOP   BELIEVE
SUCCESSFUL OUTCOME OF ENTERPRISE
ASSURED SUGGEST EARLY VISIT   WARD

The ore body the prospectors had struck measured approximately eight hundred by five hundred feet with a maximum thickness of one hundred and seventy feet. Several other significant ore deposits were subsequently uncovered in the surrounding area. Cary Mullen died a poor man in St. John's in 1922, unaware that his cooking fire had been lit almost directly above six and a half million tons of high grade ore that would net the American Smelting and Mining Company (or Uncle SAM, as the people of Black Rock would come to name it) hundreds of millions of dollars in the next half-century.

ROOTS

What he came back to:

His birth place. A town like a tree with dutch elm disease, something dying from the inside out. The wind across the barrens, whistling through telephone wires, a sound so constant it is often mistaken for silence. His parents' house. Wall to wall carpets. The formica table in the kitchen. Crocheted doilies on the coffee and end tables in the living room. His bedroom. The faded Star Wars bedspread. The window looking over the birch trees in the backyard, their branches almost touching the glass now. Barely visible beyond them, the dirty grey skirt of the mine tailings circling the huddle of mills.

For most of a decade, Ian had worked as a freelance journalist and photographer in Toronto. He thought of his hometown as something he had overcome, as if it was a childhood disease like polio. Not even his accent had survived the move to the mainland.

His father suffered his first mild stroke the previous winter, his mother's voice on the telephone touching him in a place he had almost forgotten. A nearly audible buckling passed through him, like the tremor in the air that precedes a rockfall.

"And what exactly are you planning to do with all this," his mother asks, pouring him a cup of tea and nodding her chin at his tape recorder, his packet of photographs from the Miner's Museum.

"Not sure exactly. I'm just going to see what I can dig up and go from there."

His mother sets the tea pot gently on the table, her careful motion full of a fierce energy that makes the hair on the back of Ian's neck bristle. "I don't see why you're so interested in this stuff all of a sudden," she says.

"What *stuff*?"

She waves her hand to indicate the room, the town. "You know," she says, "your *roots*." She turns away to get the tin milk from the refrigerator. "And I don't see what you hope to accomplish by making your father go through all of that again. He's not a young man anymore, you know." She stares at her son for a moment, then passes him the tin. Her silence is more familiar to Ian than her voice, rainbowed with wordless implication.

His father shuffles in from the living room where he's been napping.

"Sit down and drink your tea," his mother says. "I'll get you a tea bun and some cheese, you should eat something."

His father looks across the table at Ian. "Well, I'll never starve to death at least," he says. He looks down at the manila packet of photographs, and Ian thinks his father might just as well be staring into a mirror: black and whites of men in hard hats and coveralls, the line of muscles in the jaw tensed as they push the drill into the black rockface; constellations of dust and stone shards in the air, like confetti thrown at a wedding; miners with picks breaking up rock over an ore pass; a man staring into the funnel of the crusher. Sometimes the photos include the names of the men in the pictures, mostly they do not. *Men coming off shift*, written in ink across the back, *Miners building square set of timber in a pillar.*

"When do you want to get started on these pictures," his father says, nodding his chin towards them in exactly the same fashion his mother had.

DIGGING, A NIGHTMARE

Where the overburden was deeper than a hundred feet it was all underground mining, you see, vertical cut and fill stopes. You dig off each shaft, following the minerals, and as each stope is mined out you bring in sand to back-fill it, fence it off, and keep heading down the main shaft. It's like an artery with a series of plugged veins all along the length of it. Sometimes the fencing gives way and the sand comes out in a wave. That was what happened in '67 when Harry Follow was killed. And Clem Morgan was there, the sand took him against the rock wall and buried him up to his armpits. Two of us from stopes down the line got in with spades to clear sand. We'd dig down a foot or so, enough for him to start wiggling an arm loose, then we'd get another spill of sand coming out of the drift and we'd have to pull back and leave him there. The second time that happened, when we got back in, we couldn't see Clem anywhere. We started shouting for him as if he was hiding on us, you know, as if he was just playing a game and would answer us eventually. And then we saw the light of his headlamp, like a flashlight under a blanket. Climbed up there on our knees and started digging with our hands so as not to strike him in the head with the spades.

I've had nightmares about that ever since, about being buried alive like that. . . .

No. No, we'd given up on Harry almost from the start. Goddamn shame, and not even anyone you could blame for it you know, just one of those things. I can't say whether that makes it easier or harder to deal with.

A THUMBNAIL SKETCH

Ian's father began going underground in the Black Rock mines in 1950, at the age of nineteen. He stood six foot tall and more, his hair combed straight back from his high forehead to cover a prominent bald spot at the crown. He worked eight to fourteen hours a day, six days a week, sending money home to his mother in white letterless envelopes. He slept in No. 9 bunkhouse where the men used kerosene torches to clear vermin from the bed-springs beneath the mattresses, where the Company introduced cockroaches to deal with an infestation of ticks. He played poker until four in the morning and walked into work at eight, his head pounding with a moonshine hangover.

In 1957 he met his future wife, Joan Higden, a new teacher at the high school. At a dance at the Star Hall they sat between mutual acquaintances and barely spoke two words to one another the entire night. He was awkward and polite in a pater-nal fashion, as if he was an older man stuck in the company of teenagers. When he offered to walk her back to the teachers' residence she was too surprised to say no. The moon was out. He gave her the first verse of Byron's "She walks in beauty like the night," a poem he had been forced to memorize as a boy in school. She says it was like watching a stone catch fire.

Six months later they were married. They had two children: Ian, the eldest, and a daughter who died of Sudden Infant Death Syndrome when she was eight months old. They have not spo-ken of her in each others' company for twenty-five years.

In 1974, Ian's father was given a commendation by the American Smelting and Mining Company for his part in rescue efforts following a cave-in at the Lucky Strike mine in October of that year. In 1975, he was one of seven men and two women honored at an annual banquet for employees who had provided twenty-five years of service to the Company.

During his time at the mine, he took part in five legal and two wild cat strikes, assisted in the over-turning of a staff car that attempted to cross the picket line in 1972, and personally broke out windows in the Company office on at least two occasions. He sat on the union executive for eight years and refused a promotion to a management position in 1975.

He was laid off in 1988 after thirty-eight years of employment.

SOME GRAND IDEA

You'll probably remember the time Clay Keough got killed. That was in '74, you would've been, what? Ten or eleven by then I guess. There were six other men trapped down there, Everett King and Sandy Wilcox, Stan Caines was down there. Number 7 shaft of the Lucky Strike mine, which was the oldest mine going at the time. The ventilation system was sub-standard when it was installed and got worse over the years, but they wouldn't put out the money to fix it up properly. Blasting powder in the air, sparks flying off the equipment. There was always a chance of something setting off an explosion. Clay was killed right off, under the fall of stone and we never did get his body out of there. Took three days to reach the others, they came through an opening no bigger around than a tree stump.

[A long pause. The hiss of dead air over the tape.]

Moody Starks was one of the other fellows trapped down there, he used to carve knick-knacks, little boats and such, before the arthritis got to his hands. Gave you one for Christmas one year, you probably don't remember. He'd stare at a block of wood until he broke a sweat, then he'd start carving. He used to say, "The boat's already in there, you just have to keep whittling away until you find it." I used to laugh at that kind of talk, thought it was some grand idea, you know, just foolishness. But that's what it was like going after those men. We had no idea if they were alive or dead, you see, we just had to keep believing they were in there somewhere, waiting for us. I still feel guilty about Clay sometimes. You can't help it, I s'pose. If we'd done more, or worked harder. . . . No logic to it of course, Clay was dead before we got down the shaft, and it's no secret who was to blame.

That's what I can't understand still, how they just didn't give a fuck. I knew they were at fault, the union knew it. But the Company simply would not admit it. And who remembers that now? By and by we'll all be gone and they'll have got away with it. You write that down, you tell people. We should have burned the whole goddamn place to the ground back then.

A THUMBNAIL SKETCH (2)

On September 1st, 1928, only twenty-five days behind schedule, the Black Rock mine began operations. The first concentrates were produced in the milling facilities on September 6th, and shipped to Botwood harbour enroute to *Metallgesellschaft A. G.* of Germany. *Metallgesellschaft* and several other German companies continued to be the primary customer for Black Rock ore throughout the 1930s.

A second mine was collared in May of 1932, and began production by 1935. A seven thousand foot drift connected the two mines, and ore from the second operation was shunted to the Lucky Strike shaft to be hoisted to the mill at the surface. Less than a year later, the American Smelting and Mining Company had recouped its initial investment, with profits of over seven million dollars in less than ten years, despite the precipitous drop in the market price per ton brought on by the Depression.

All contracts with German companies were cancelled upon the British declaration of war in September, 1939. The production of metals was declared strategic to the war effort by Britain, and the Black Rock mines operated at above capacity through to 1945. Close to two dozen people from Black Rock enlisted and fought overseas during the war. Eleven were killed in action.

Further finds of smaller ore bodies in the 1950s ensured the survival of the town well into the 1970s. Between 1928 and 1977, the Black Rock mines employed between four hundred and eight hundred people in its underground and mill operations. In its sixty year history, twenty-nine men were fatally injured in mine and mill accidents. Hundreds of others were infected with silicosis, or Black Lung Disease, particularly before dry drilling was replaced by wet drilling in the early 1950s.

By the mid 80s, the majority of workers had been laid off by the Company. The last train shipment of ore left Black Rock on June 30th, 1984, after which the tracks were torn up and the ties sold off for firewood. Concentrate continued to be shipped to the harbour in Botwood by truck for another four years, until the mine was officially closed in 1988 after producing over twenty million tonnes of high grade ore.

A DISCOVERY, ITS CONSEQUENCES (2)

Ian spent hours that August and September sifting through Company records that had been donated to the local mine museum. Every evening, just before closing at six, he took a seat at a desk from the old Company offices and the museum manager would leave him to the boxes of shipment records, lists of tonnage and percentages, telexes from Company headquarters in New York, reports on equipment malfunctions. A slag heap of information, the yellowed papers breaking into dust motes under his fingers. He stared at the intricate rootwork of faded handwriting until he was dizzy, his left hand absently worrying the bald spot at the back of his head. The only thing that kept him going was the occasional appearance of his father's name in payment records, on a list of employees receiving a watch for twenty-five years of service.

Then, on a Saturday evening in late September, this reference in a Shift Boss log:

February 25th, 1950
4:20pm

Accident involving railway car from shaft 17, at the hoist. Crew being taken to cage after day shift, on way to surface. Dick Lane exited car before complete stop, fell between car and loading ramp. In serious condition when brought to surface, ambulance contacted immediately. Three other men in car at time of accident— Harold Yetman, Charlie Cooke, Paul Neary—questioned by shift boss and sent home. Waiting for news from hospital re: Lane's condition. Further investigation pending.

4:30pm

Lane pronounced dead on arrival at hospital.

Ian read and re-read the entry, the name of the dead man, the date, the names of the other men in the car. He made a photo-copy of the report and carried it home, kneeling beside his father's chair to point out his name between Harold Yetman's and Paul Neary's. "I can't find another Charlie Cooke in the records," he said. "I thought you said you weren't on shift when this happened?"

His father fingered the paper so the ends curled up like the pages of a book left out in the rain. His mouth was working, the click of his false teeth like an old clock keeping bad time.

"Dad?"

His mother came into the room with a glass of water and

a handful of pills cupped in her palm. "Time for your medication," she said and his father pushed the paper away, dismissing the question. His mother touched her husband's forehead as he brought the glass of water to his mouth, his hand trembling slightly with age. "Are you alright?" she asked him. "You look a little pale."

"Stop being such a bloody nursemaid," his father said, trying to rise quickly from the chair and stumbling. "I'm alright!" he shouted when Ian and his mother reached for him. He left the room then, climbing the stairs as firmly as he was able.

"What were you two talking about?" his mother asked.

"Nothing," Ian said, folding the paper into his back pocket. "Some things about the mine is all."

A pained look worried his mother's face, as if her tongue had just touched a canker on the inside of her mouth. "You know what I told you about all this," she said.

"I don't know what got into him," Ian said. He shrugged.

His mother looked down at the backs of her hands and an expression of impatience crossed her face. "I hope," she said to him, and then paused. "I hope," she said, trying to smile, to be more conciliatory, "that you finish this book or whatever it is before your father goes. Because I don't want how he dies to be in there. I'll have to go through it once and that will be just about enough for me, thank you very much."

The next morning Ian took his camera onto what used to be Company property, walking among the maze of ash grey buildings, the doors of the mills padlocked, signs warning of danger posted at every entrance, the high dark windows like the eyes of a dead animal. At the same time, his father sat in the United Church, listening to the minister's voice become a nest of bees in the rafters, then collapsing forward and sideways onto the floor.

AN ACT OF GOD (2)

From a Report of the Independent Inquiry into the Lucky Strike Rock Fall, housed with the Management Files of the American Smelting and Mining Company (Black Rock Operations), at the Black Rock Miner's Museum:

It is the conclusion of this Inquiry, after considering evidence and testimony from Company, union and government sources, that the rock fall at the Lucky Strike Mine which occurred on October 28th, 1974, was an Act of God; further that the American Smelting and Mining Company and its managers are in no way responsible for the accident or its unfortunate consequences.

While the Inquiry does acknowledge the concern expressed by union representatives about conditions in the Numbers 5, 7, 8 and 11 shafts of the Lucky Strike mine, we find that conditions in these shafts, and the foreseeable hazards of these conditions, were well within normal industry and legislative standards at the time of the accident. The root causes of the rock fall are not directly attributable to negligence or human error.

It is the opinion of this Inquiry that there is no basis for the pursuit of criminal charges related to this incident, and that further investigation of this matter would be neither necessary, nor helpful.

DIGGING: A NIGHTMARE

A dark tunnel, the sound of water dripping and echoing. There's no light but the pale beam from his own forehead. A wave of sand is swirled along one side of the tunnel and he is looking for someone there, walking the length of the tunnel and shouting a name. When he reaches the far end of the darkness, there's a dull glow visible beneath the sand. He clambers to the top of the small dune and begins digging frantically with his hands. He clears the sand away from a face and realizes it's his father he's been looking for, his father he is unearthing.

His father's eyes are closed. He can't tell if he's dead or alive, but in a panic he begins covering the face again, pushing handfuls of sand over the rigid, unexpressive features. He is still burying his father when he wakes in a chair beside the hospital bed.

SOME GRAND IDEA (2)

The doctor examines his father briefly, listening to his heart, pulling an eyelid down to look at his pupil. He straightens and smiles a stiff smile. "He's stable for now," he announces. "We can send him home in a few days if things improve. There's no reason to keep him here any longer than we have to."

Ian considers the weight of the doctor's words. He can't help interpreting them as bad news: it's just a matter of time; there's nothing the hospital can do to help.

"I warned you about this," his mother says after the doctor leaves the room. She's sitting rigid in her chair beside the bed, staring past her husband. "I told you what could happen." Her scalp shows through her fine thin hair, so white it almost appears to be glowing.

"This is not my fault," Ian whispers.

"Don't pretend innocence with me," she says. "Coming back after all this time with some grand idea of yourself. Rooting into things you don't understand."

Ian's father has barely spoken a word in the days since his collapse, his voice weak and slurred, fading in and out like a stray radio signal. He lifts a finger in the direction of the people beside the bed now and they both stand and come closer, his wife taking his hand in hers.

"Dick," Ian's father says, distinctly.

"Shhh," his wife whispers. "Don't try to speak."

Ian's father shakes his head on the pillow. "Dick Lane," he says. "1950."

"Charlie, you don't have to do this now." His mother's voice beginning to quaver, like a divining rod over water.

"No," his father says, turning toward Ian. "End of the shift, see. Racing to get to the hoist. Just kids then, nineteen or twenty. Dick was at the front of the rail car, Harold Yetman next to him pushing to get by."

"You don't have to do this," his mother says again.

"No," his father says, still watching his son. "No. Write this down. Harold pushed him is what happened. We lied about it, said he fell. Blood in his lungs. *I'm drowning* he kept saying, *Let me up, I'm drowning.*"

Ian's mother turns away from the bed and her husband

looks at her back with his eyes, as if he's unable to move his head.

Ian shrugs helplessly. He'd been expecting something far worse, he realizes, a darker secret, and the relief he feels makes him giggle stupidly. "Mom," he says, "it's not that big a deal."

She turns back toward the bed, but refuses to look at her son. "You would think so," she says.

ROOTS (2)

The fluorescent light from the bathroom throws shadows into his parents' bedroom. From where Ian stands in the doorway he can see his father's face, white against the pillowcase, the pale white of roots, of creatures that live their whole lives underground. His long unexpressive features are like something carved out of wood, a permanent scaffolding of lines around his eyes from peering in poor light. He lies motionless in his bed beneath the weight of the thin sheets.

His father could die in the night, Ian figures, or he might hang on for years still, like the town. He listens for the soft hiss of breathing across the room, a grunt or snore, some kind of reassurance. He misses the hospital heart monitor, its quiet, comforting blip, the jagged graph on the screen like the rise and fall of a company's stocks. He can hear the faint clatter of cups and saucers in the kitchen downstairs, the kettle whistling to a boil. After she pours the water, his mother will call him down for tea and he waits for her voice before he turns away.

FLESH

May 26th, 1989

She heard footsteps on the front bridge, the heavy shrug of the door. "Any chance of a cup of tea here this morning?" Angus shouted into the house. As if he expected to find everyone still in bed.

Peg swore under her breath. "Gary's at work," she shouted back.

Angus came into the kitchen and stood beside the table, his good hand resting lightly on the back of a chair. He had a slack, stunned expression on his face. "Work?" He was wearing a red plaid lumberjack shirt and work pants; the laces of his steel-toed boots were undone, the greasy leather tongues lolling loose.

Peg turned away from him and wiped absently at the kitchen counter with the dish rag. "Started on one of those government projects," she explained, "painting the hospital."

He shrugged and sat down, laying his hands on the table top. He had rearranged his expression quickly, the way he might have hastily thrown the covers over a bed with unexpected visitors at the door. "You've made a cup of tea in your time I s'pose, have you?"

Angus was on permanent disability since the accident and he spent his days wandering from one house to another looking for company. After Gary was laid off, Angus made their place a semi-regular stop on his rounds. Most people found it difficult to remain civil around him because of his ways and his drinking, but Gary avoided conflict at all costs and they had become friends of a sort as a result. He offered Angus tea, pickled eggs and cold bologna sandwiches, an occasional snort, something close to a sympathetic ear.

Peg on the other hand made herself scarce whenever he came through the door, throwing on her coat and running across the road to sit with Linda Troke. Gary could see her at Linda's kitchen table, watching through the curtains for Angus to leave. He couldn't understand the animosity Peg felt for the man. When he asked her to explain it, Peg called Angus a pathetic little cradle robber.

"Jesus Christ, Peg," Gary said. "What does that make me then?"

She shrugged. "You're different."

"I'm different." He nodded emphatically to underline the inadequacy of this distinction.

Angus never said a word to Gary about Peg's absence, although he was so preoccupied with his marital problems that he rarely talked of anything else. It was reasonable to think that this single-minded, drunken self-pity was enough in and of itself to make Peg want to avoid the man and she wished Gary could leave it at that.

By the time she'd set a mug of tea in front of him, Angus had already started in about Bev leaving him, as if Peg was a long-time and trusted confidant. He clutched his mug with the thumb and finger of his ruined hand. The woman, he announced, was as cold as an outhouse seat in the dead of winter, she'd gone off sex after the first baby and wouldn't sleep with him at all the last two years they were together. She got half his pension in the settlement and the two kids on top of that. Every item in the list brought Angus closer to snivelling, tears welling up behind the Coke-bottle lenses of his glasses, his eyes like two helpless infant creatures still wet with afterbirth.

They hadn't sat alone in one another's company since she was a teenager. His thin hair was combed to the side, the part revealing a crooked line of unhealthy scalp. He wore long mossy sideburns that hadn't been in style since she was a child. *Flesh of my flesh*, she thought. He'd probably already had a drink, or several, by now, she knew, and it made her frantic to hear him go on. After fifteen minutes she left him at the table to strip the beds upstairs, collect laundry, sweep dust from beneath furniture, scour the tub and toilet, straighten closets.

The diary was stored away at the bottom of a box filled with old school textbooks, photograph albums, a dried wedding corsage, letters bound with ribbon. For a moment she didn't recognize it. It had a bright floral plastic cover and a clasp. Inside, there were more than a hundred pages in her tiny, secretive script. She'd kept it faithfully through her teens, tracking the daily patterns of her family's world like someone obsessed with recording the predictable vagaries of the weather: what they ate, which shows they watched, who came by during the day.

Her four oldest siblings had already moved out into jobs and marriages by then, but someone was always dropping by around suppertime and they ate in shifts to have room at the kitchen table. The single bathroom was continually under siege, daily arguments erupted over the television, over who was sitting in whose spot on the chesterfield. The diary had been the only private place in her life for years. She turned to the last entry, pages from the end of the book.

Babysat for Bev tonight. She was wearing her blue dress from Simpsons. Watched Laugh-In, Dukes of Hazard (repeat). Home by one-thirty.

The blue dress. Bev.

All that empty space between the letters.

October 10th, 1976

They were upstairs getting dressed when she arrived, the baby already down for the night and sleeping. Seconds after she came in the door there was the sound of Angus' shoes on the stairs, *click click click*. She sat at the kitchen table, opened the book she'd brought with her and bowed her head studiously to the page.

"She'll be an hour yet," Angus said sourly. He went to the counter to fix himself a whiskey. "Kettle's still warm. Cup of tea?"

She didn't look up. He put the kettle on the element, then sat at the table across from her with his glass. She could smell aftershave, soap, a faint but acrid undertone of sulphur from the mill. His unharmed fingers drummed the table top.

"Good book?"

He was eyeing her get-up, the baggy sweatshirt, the loose track pants. The thick lenses of his glasses made her feel he could see right through her clothes. When she didn't answer him, he said, "You didn't have to get all made up to come over here, you know."

She shrugged.

"That's not how you used to dress," he said slyly, sipping his whiskey. "Those jeans of yours," he said, "there ought to be a law. And those t-shirts. You've already got more up top than the wife does."

She turned the page. Folded her arms firmly across her chest.

"Oh well, more than a handful's a waste, that's what I say. She goes snakey when I suck on them." He held up his hand. "Just have to use the one finger to bring her off sometimes." The kettle shook on the stove, the spout spitting a white column of steam.

Bev came down the stairs and Peg looked up from her book as she stepped into the kitchen. The blue dress hugged her belly, the white strap of her bra showing on the shoulder. Her breasts were the size of small apples. She crossed the kitchen and stood beside Peg, a hand casually placed on the nape of her neck. "Whatcha reading?" she asked.

Angus got up and switched off the stove element with a small furious twist of his wrist. "We're late already, never-mind jawing. You can make yourself a cup, I s'pose, can you?" he said.

Bev pulled on a raglan in the tiny porch. "Back by one," she said, with a private look of apology for her husband's mood. Then they were gone.

1972

In their last years of high school Bev had been best friends with Peg's sister Angela, and Bev spent most of every weekend at their house. Peg's father, Pious, called her the "star boarder" and complained about her being constantly underfoot, about how much food she ate. Bev called him Dad. "You should be so frigging lucky," he'd say. But he didn't mind having her around—one more or less made no appreciable difference—and he enjoyed the novelty of her teasing, affectionate title for him. His own children simply called him by his Christian name, which he had never been particularly fond of.

Peg's mother, Mary, had grown considerably less strict with her children as the oldest became adults and moved out on their own, as if she was happy to have shepherded a few offspring safely into their own lives and was too tired to fight the rest. She presided over the family in her housecoat and knitted slippers like a shop-worn but benevolent queen. Bev and Ange spent all their time at the house because Mary ignored them when they swore, as long as they didn't use the F-word, and never complained when they stacked forty-fives on the record player and danced around the coffee table. When Pious and the boys were outside sawing and stowing firewood, Mary let them smoke with her in the living room.

Peg was twelve years old, the last of eleven children. For most of her young life she felt like the tail of a dog. She was largely ignored by her brothers and sisters, and she'd learned to participate passively in the lives of the people around her, as if she was part of the audience at a play.

She and Angela shared a narrow bedroom with two single cots. Peg could sit on the edge of one and rest her feet on the other. She flopped on the bed next to the wall pretending to read a book while Ange and Bev sat opposite beside the window, blowing smoke through the vent and discussing who they were in love with lately, who they'd allowed to get how far, who would never be permitted to lay a finger on them. Peg couldn't quite figure the rules of this game, how they offered or withheld their bodies piece by piece according to an obscure calculation of affection and risk. But she aspired to their precocious confidence.

"That frigger Andy Loder tried to get his hand under my bra when we were out at the trestle," Ange said. "He got a good poke in the balls for his trouble."

Bev gave the puke sign with her index finger. "Not the kind of poke he had in mind probably. Did you know Beryl Scaines let him do it down by the pump house last summer?"

Ange hushed up suddenly, as if she had just sighted an intruder. She gestured toward Peggy with her chin. "She's not reading over there, you know," she warned Bev. "Watch what you say because all of this will end up in that book of hers."

"Shut up, Ange," Peg said without looking up.

"What book?"

"Her di-a-reee. What do you think she's doing all that time in the bathroom with the door locked? Di-a-ree-ah," she sang derisively.

"Oh, Peg, my lover," Bev said, "all along I thought you were in the tub with your feet up beside the taps."

"Like she'd know enough to try that," Angela snorted.

Peggy stared resolutely at her book. She didn't know exactly what the girls meant about the tub, but she could tell the kind of thing that was being implied and the intimacy of it embarrassed and excited her. The peculiar stirring between her legs was a luxurious discomfort, but also vaguely threatening, it attracted and repelled her in equal measure. Her flesh was covered in goosebumps.

On Friday nights the girls went to teenage dances at the rink or the Boys' and Girls' Club. Peg's mother, despite her laxness in almost all other areas of parenting, refused to let Peggy join them before she turned thirteen. She waited up for them, listening for their stifled laughter on the stairs when they arrived. More often than not, they had been drinking and stumbled into the bedroom in a rowdy mood, bouncing on the mattresses, blowing farts on the bare skin of their arms like boys.

Ange had necked with Hayward O'Brien during the last song of the night. Bev danced with moony Cyril Veitch out of pity and the boy's immediate erection made it difficult to shuffle the tiny circle required.

"I told you what would happen," Ange shrugged. "You looked like a frigging hunchback."

"Well I didn't want it to *touch* me," Bev said indignantly. "Jesus, Mary and Joseph."

They squeezed together into the tiny bed under the window until Ange sat up in a fit of giggles. "Keep your hands off me you lezzie, go sleep with Peg."

Peg rolled into the warmth of the older girl's arms when Bev crawled under the covers, slipping a bare leg between her thighs. A small lake of heat. She loved the intimacy of Bev's naked smell radiating through the dull halo of cigarette smoke and liquor on her breath. The alcohol made Bev affectionate in a casually physical way; she stroked Peg's back, leaned down to kiss her forehead. Peg rested her face against the bare skin of Bev's neck, her nose touching the hollow at the base of her throat. Her nipples so erect they hurt.

Dear Diary, she wrote the next day, locked safely in the bathroom, *Bev stayed over last night. Ange called her a lezzie but I think she's beautiful.*

There was a loud rap at the door. "Come on," Pious shouted. "You can't stay in there all the jesus morning."

1974–76

Angus was twenty-six years old and had already suffered through a short painful marriage when he began dating Bev. Peggy wasn't quite seven when he first moved out of the house and started work at the ore mill. She had no idea what happened to his first marriage beyond whispers about another man. He'd gone through a bad time of drinking and public grief that had almost cost him his job. For a long period, he didn't visit the house at all.

When he began coming around again, he paid unusual attention to his youngest sister, taking her out to Hardy's in the pick-up to stow a load of lumber for the cabin he was building at the lake, instigating long games of crib at the kitchen table and deliberately losing. He smiled broadly at her when she pegged the last two points to skunk him for the third game in a row. Behind the thick lenses of his glasses his oddly magnified eyes seemed to glow with inordinate brotherly affection. Peg was flattered in a shy, suspicious way. It was the first time an adult had consciously courted her company, and she was sure there was some ulterior motive.

Bev.

What was she like? Angus wanted to know. What kinds of things did she talk about? What music did she listen to? Did she have a boyfriend? For a time Peg thought she was the one driving these conversations, constantly steering their talk back to the one topic she never tired of. Eventually, though, she began to feel curiously exposed, picked over, like a carcass diligently attended by a fox, and she quickly became more reticent. "Cat got your tongue?" he teased her, and she blushed, shaking her head furiously as if she was trying to avoid a kiss.

Once he and Bev began going out, Angus' relationship with Peg settled into its old pattern of distant, myopic affection. Bev moved off into a world that was beyond the horizon of Peg's knowledge and imagination: drinking parties on the beach at Beothuk Lake; adult dances at the Legion Hall.

Angela sat with Peg in the tiny bedroom, cursing Angus for the sneaking dog he was and slagging Bev for being fool enough to fall for him. She had been dumped and she wasn't happy about it. She offered Peg an occasional drag on her cigarette. "Angus is a pathetic little cradle-robber," Ange told her sister. "You can put that down in your book if you like, you can quote me on it."

They both stood at the wedding, along with Bev's sister. They wore pink taffeta dresses that made them look pale and unhappy. The priest read a passage from Genesis: *Therefore a man leaves his father and his mother and cleaves to his wife and they become one flesh.* At the reception, the bridal bouquet was caught by an eight-year-old girl which put Angela into a funk for the rest of the evening. At three in the morning, the newly-weds left the party to begin a week-long honeymoon at Angus' recently completed cabin on Beothuk Lake.

Angela and Bev never recovered. They carried on a perfunctory friendship for months after the wedding, but the casual solidarity that once defined them was gone. Peg dropped by the new couple's place for tea after school, spent an occasional Friday night with them watching made-for-TV movies, and Angus, who credited Peg in some small way with helping him land his wife, was buoyant and generous in her company. He called Peg the "star boarder" with his father's good-natured sarcasm and sat by himself in the living room to allow his wife and sister time alone. And as Bev came to the realization that her marriage was going to be a lonelier place than she'd expected, she turned to Peg. They spent afternoons baking molasses bread or raisin buns and gossiping. They stacked 45s on the stereo and danced around the coffee table. One Saturday night Bev got Peg drunk on Grasshoppers and explained what "feet up beside the taps" was all about. Peg fell off her chair laughing.

When Angus was on shift they hiked out past the dam to the trestle, then walked the Penstock down to the power house, smoking cigarettes and talking. The huge water pipeline was covered in decades of graffiti: peace signs, hearts and arrows, *Ben luvs Vicki 1963, Charmaine and Ches 4 Ever.* They found Angus' name intimately connected to the name of his first wife and Bev vowed to return with a can of paint to put things right, but never got around to it.

Bev liked to make a show of Peg's developing body, reliving

the unattached promise of her adolescence through her younger friend. They spent hours in the bedroom, Peg stripped to her underwear and draped with outfits Bev thought might flatter her figure. "You're going to be a heartbreaker," Bev said, looking over Peg's shoulder into the mirror, her arms linked loosely around her waist. Angus sometimes walked in on them and smiled paternally. "My two favourite women," he said. Peg daydreamed about moving in with them once she turned eighteen.

February 17th, 1984

Peg's third child was just two and a half months old. The oldest was away at school, Mattie was down for a nap. She had the infant at her breast, watching the tiny face search for the nipple, the toothless mouth closing with greedy tenacity when he found it. It made her think of Gary's mouth there the night before, of how gentle he had been, how generous. It was the first time they had made love since the birth, which had been complicated and difficult, and he was so afraid of causing her pain that he wouldn't enter her, kissing his way down her body instead, lying between her legs until she came.

Mary had always said that Peg fell in love with Gary because he was so much like Pious. She tried to imagine her parents engaged in a similar "exercise," but the thought of it made her laugh out loud. They must have done something to have eleven kids, she was willing to grant that, but certain activities seemed completely out of the realm of possibility.

It was a clear, cold day, the trees stiff with frost. She sat near the window, the pale yellow circle of the winter sun hanging low on the horizon, warming herself and the child. She wanted the whole day to go on like this, her and the baby in the sunlight and her head full of Gary. But there were footsteps on the front bridge, the door scraped open and closed. "I'm in the living room," she called without looking up.

Gary came through the kitchen still wearing his coat and boots, leaving a trail of snow on the linoleum. He was supposed to be on shift until four. His face was grey. "There's been an accident," he said.

Peg started to raise herself out of her chair. "Pious?" The baby's mouth lost the nipple and began crying.

"No, fuck no, sit down. It was Angus. He got his hand caught in the conveyer belt coming down from the deckhead."

Peg leaned back into the chair. She felt an overwhelming sense of relief, and then a hard knot of anger congealing in her stomach. "He's alright," she said.

"He'll be lucky if he doesn't lose his hand. The belt tore off three of the fingers, I had to dig them out from underneath with a stick. Carried them over to the hospital in a cup but I doubt they'll be any use. Christ, what a mess."

Peg thought of the hand Angus had held up for her to see, the things he told her those fingers had done. She looked down at the baby as he settled back to nursing. She said, "He was drunk, wasn't he."

Gary shook his head. "Of course he was drunk," he said. He sat heavily on the chesterfield.

"And no one's going to say a thing about it, are they?" Peg looked away out the window. A blue car rolled down the street with the slow pendulous grace of a raindrop on a pane of glass. "You shouldn't have to lie for him," she said.

"For fuck sake, woman," Gary whispered, "he's your own flesh and blood." She turned her head toward him and as she did she saw Gary's face darken, as if a cloud had moved across the sun lighting the room. "Peg, will you tell me what happened between you two?"

She turned away again, shaking her head. "Nothing," she said. "Nothing happened."

He stood up beside her in his bulky winter coat and grabbed the back of the chair she was sitting in. "Jesus, Peg, did he ever touch you?"

There was such an unfamiliar current of fury in her husband's voice that Peg began crying.

"I'm sorry," he said, sitting back on the chesterfield. "Don't cry, for the love of Christ. I didn't mean. . . ."

"He never laid a hand on me Gary. Never."

He nodded his head emphatically, to appease her, to let her know there was nothing more she had to say.

June 11th, 1978

Halfway down the Penstock they stopped for a smoke.

They'd left the baby with Mary and Pious for the afternoon. Angus was at home alone and was probably into the bottle already, although it was only two o'clock. Drinking that early in the day made him moody, ridiculously boisterous or silent in a dark way, and Bev was in no rush to get back.

It was a still summer day, the air clotted with the whine of black flies. Peg sat up top, the metal surface ripe with the sun's heat, warming her bottom through her jeans. She could hear the sound of the waterfall at the Mudhole among the trees below them, and the shouting and laughter of swimmers. Bev jumped down off the pipeline and began reading the graffiti aloud while she smoked. *Francis and Vera May '62, Peace Not War, Pot Pot Pot Pot, Faye M loves Clayton S.*

She had just told Peg that she was pregnant with a second child. Peg was walking behind her on the Penstock, watching her feet to keep to the centre of the pipe, Bev talking without turning her head. "The one time we screwed the whole month without a frigging rubber," she'd said.

Peg watched Bev standing below her now, holding her cigarette like a tiny baton, and she felt a sudden and overwhelming dislike for the woman. It upset her to think of Angus touching her in the way he said he did, to think that she let him do these things. That she enjoyed them. The thought of Bev's nipples in her brother's mouth, of his fingers touching her "down there," spoiled Bev's beauty for her. She tried to forget these details, to pretend the words had never been spoken at all, but they stayed with her like burrs in an animal's fur.

Bev bent from the waist to read something scrawled on the underside of the pipe. *"Beryl Scaines is a whore."* She straightened and looked up at Peg. "Is she ever," she said and shook her head.

Peg stood up and began walking away. "Hey," Bev shouted after her. "Give us a hand would you?" She was trying to jump up onto the Penstock, sliding helplessly back to the ground after each effort. "Peg," she shouted.

Peggy stopped to look back at her. "You should talk," she said. Her voice sounded pathetic, cruel and helplessly needy all at once. Hearing it made her angrier than she already was, and she turned and kept walking.

May 26th, 1989

When she came downstairs Angus was asleep on the chester-field, his glasses set on the floor beside him. He'd thrown an arm over his face, his left leg was cocked and splayed awk-wardly to the side as if it was broken. He was snoring gently and looked so completely vulnerable that Peg felt she could hurt him as easily as she could an infant. She thought of how this morning would have been recorded in her diary: *Angus came by before ten, stayed for tea. Would not shut up about Bev. Fell asleep on the chesterfield.* So matter of fact it would almost be meaningless.

And maybe that was as close to the truth as a person could get, she thought, maybe it was kidding yourself to flesh it out any more than that. But something shifted as she stood beside him, she felt her heart nudge slightly forward, like a heavy door pushed by a child. The poor, pitiful bastard. He'd fought as hard as he knew how to keep Bev for himself and still he'd lost her.

She turned to walk into the kitchen and her brother stirred as she passed, sitting up suddenly. He didn't seem to know where he was and he patted his pockets wildly, squinting blind-ly around the room until he picked out Peg's blurred figure and stared, trying to make out who she was. Peg couldn't remember ever seeing him without his glasses. His naked eyes looked too small for his face.

THE NIGHT WATCHMAN

Darkness wakes me. The moons rise at the tips of my fingers. I stare out the window, watching lights nip out in houses up and down the street. By eleven the town looks deserted. On the other side of the world, the sun is up. Awake, like me, but with more company.

Sometimes I go upstairs to my bed and watch the ceiling. Sometimes I pull on my boots and walk for hours. I could make my way through town with my eyes closed, circling my stations like a blind horse on its milk route: the mill, the train shed, the core shacks, then down Bennett's Hill to the bunkhouse, past Ellen's old place at the foot of Main Street. I suppose it was those years of shift work, of sleeping through daylight that keeps me up now. For thirty years I was the night watchman in Black Rock.

Walking the streets of a town at night you get to see the soft underbelly of people's lives. It was a lonely job. I knew too much about everyone: which couples were up fighting in the middle of the night; who was sneaking from the bunkhouse to meet a married woman, or a girl not yet eighteen, out by the trestle; who stumbled bleary-eyed and hungover on their way to work just minutes before the whistle blew.

Occasionally, I learned more than I wanted to know and the knowing crawled under my skin and burrowed in there. Maybe it's that remembering makes the night so hard to get through.

What needs to be understood is this: when I reported Stick Walker to the Company I was just doing my job.

I was making my second round of the shift that night, a little before one in the morning. There were lights in the windows of the laundry as I came around Bennet's Hill, which was nothing unusual. The Chinaman was up that late as a rule, often later, working by the light of kerosene lamps, and he'd already stoked the fire for the irons by the time I did my last round at seven am. I'd never spoken to him beyond dropping off and picking up my clothes, but I felt I knew him better than most. I waved to him from the street as I walked by and he nodded without looking up from his work. We were each a marker in the other's schedule, as predictable as the Company whistle bracketing shifts.

As I came closer to the building that night I heard a fuss inside, two voices arguing, a man's drunken laughter, and I began walking more quickly toward the one-storey shack. "C'mon you fucker," someone was insisting, "have a *dlink* with me, have a fucking *dlink*."

Both men turned guiltily in my direction when I came in, as if I had caught them kissing. They were standing beside one another, and Stick was holding Wah Lee's dark blue shirt at the shoulder. He was almost a foot taller than the Chinaman and he looked like he was scolding a child. The air in the room was thick with steam and the smell of laundry blueing. Shirts and pants hung to dry on clothes lines across the room, like empty skins. When he realized who I was Stick let go of Wah Lee's shirt. He made a clumsy attempt to push a silver flask into the inside pocket of his coat, but it fell to the floor with a thunk. We all stared at it there, lying on its back like a turtle with its belly exposed.

"What's going on here?" I said.

Wah Lee shook his head vigorously. "Mister Stick just leaving," he said. "Good night, good night." He waved with both hands toward the door, shooing us outside, but nobody moved. Stick pulled out a cigarette and lit it, dropping the match to the floor where it burnt down to the end before going out. Finally I stepped forward and picked up the flask, slipping it into my coat pocket.

"Stick," I told him, "you'd best be getting back to the bunkhouse."

"Me and the Chinaman were just having a chat," Stick said, a mouthful of smoke escaping his lips with each word. "No concern of yours Mr. Watchman."

"I mean it Stick," I said.

He raised his hands above his shoulders and nodded his head. "Alright, Mr. Watchman, sir," he said. "Don't have to get upset about this. Nothing to get upset about, is there Chinaman?" He made his way to the door and turned to back through, winking at Wah Lee and myself before stepping outside into darkness.

Wah Lee bent to pick up the black stub of the match from the floor. "Mr. Stick no trouble," he told me. "I don't want no trouble."

"I'll take care of this," I said.

"I don't want no trouble."

"Don't worry about it," I told him, and I left then to make sure Stick was on his way to the bunkhouse.

———————

The night watchman's job, as I understood it, was simply to watch and record. "Don't get involved," I was told when I started. "Keep an eye on things, but stay clear where you can. You don't break up fights or get in the middle of arguments. You're just an observer, understand? See anything out of order, you bring the report to us and we'll take it from there."

Some observations from my first year as night watchman: the sidewalks on Main Street were made of wooden slats, the roads were ankle deep in mud during spring and fall; the Black Rock Miners senior men's hockey team won the Herder Memorial Trophy over the St. John's Capitals for the second year in a row; the Company cut the lights from midnight until seven, leaving power on only for the mills and a sparse crop of streetlamps; Wah Lee's wife arrived from China to live with him in Black Rock late that August.

Trivial details when you set them out bald like that, and separate from one another. I've lived alone all my life for no reason I can single out, although I know some combination of these insignificant details is partially to blame.

No one can remember when Wah Lee came to Black Rock, or how he ended up here. Some say that when he arrived on the train he couldn't manage a single word of English, a piece of paper pinned to his lapel addressing him like a parcel: "Wah Lee, Black Rock by way of Black Rock Jct." The men in the bunkhouses brought him their work clothes and long underwear, exchanging them for stubs of paper inscribed with a horizontal row of Chinese characters. They kept the ticket on a nail over their beds, having learned that Wah Lee meant business when he said "No ticket, no crothes." He never smiled, bent over the irons on the stove or the row of steaming wash tubs as soon as he had written your stub or returned your laundry, silently dismissing you.

After his wife arrived from China, Wah Lee seemed to withdraw even further into himself, as if he was going back to his own country in his mind. It was a rare thing to lay eyes on his wife at all, she kept herself hidden away in a room at the back of the laundry. There were a dozen rumours about her making the rounds that year. People said that it cost Wah Lee every cent he had to bring her here, that for a while they were reduced to boiling and eating grass because they had no money for food. They said that Mrs. Lee was "not herself" and made life hell for the Chinaman; that she refused to drink or cook with water from the taps, convinced that it was poisoned, and forced Wah Lee to carry buckets down to the brook below their house at six each morning to fetch their daily supply.

Four times a night I walked down Bennet's Hill to clock in at the bunkhouse station, passing Wah Lee's laundry. More often than not I could hear the low wail of a woman's voice from the back room, a wounded sound like something a trapped animal might make. Sometimes I heard Wah Lee's voice as well, speaking his own language or simply cooing as you would to a child, trying to offer some sort of comfort.

Some would claim I had it in for Stick Walker and I won't deny that I was happy to make my report to the foreman. Drunkenness, especially public drunkenness, was frowned upon by the Company. Anyone else would have been shipped out of town on the next train with orders given to officials in the Junction not to allow them beyond that point if they tried to return. But I knew things would be different with Stick.

The Company brought him in from Kirkland Lake, Ontario to play with the Black Rock Miners. Officially he was employed in the machine shop, where I worked before taking the job as night watchman. In reality he was paid to play hockey. Stick showed up when he felt like it and didn't do much when he did. "Kennedy," he'd say to the Shift Boss, limping into the shop two hours late, "I'm not up to work today. Stomach ache," he'd say. Headache. Bad back, sore shoulder. On his way out the door he'd wink at the rest of us bent over our machines and then step through into the light of the day.

I knew nothing much would come of my report. A slap on the wrist at most. But in my eyes, that was better than nothing. Less than an hour after I spoke with my foreman that morning two men were sent to the bunkhouse. They dragged Stick out of bed, escorted him to the machine shop and put him to work on the grinding stone, sharpening the metal bits for the underground drills. Dog work. Your hands going numb from the vibrations, your eyes watering from staring at the spinning stone.

Fair enough, I thought. It looked good on the smug son of a bitch. My job didn't make me any friends, but occasionally it brought a certain amount of personal satisfaction. I went to the mess hall where I ate a huge breakfast. Then I went to my bed and slept straight through until suppertime.

———————

I suppose something more needs to be said about Ellen, although it's only in my own head that she's a part of this story at all.

She lived with her parents in a house at the bottom of Main Street. For a short time I knew the place well, called regularly, shared meals with the family, played Crib and Crazy Eights in the living room. I took her to movies at the theatre on Saturday evenings, to the bowling hall on Wednesdays. I thought I might ask her to marry me one day and I took the job as night watchman for the raise, began saving for a ring.

From her bedroom window she looked out over the Company stables and the tail end of Bennett's Hill road leading to the bunkhouses. She waited there each night until I had passed by on my first round, her hand against the darkness of the pane. She may have loved me, I'll never know for sure now. For a long time I regretted not knowing and wouldn't forgive myself for making the decision I made. Even after she married and moved into her own place I watched for her at that window. But the farther I move away from it the more inevitable it seems that things happened the way they did.

All through that winter Mrs. Lee's illness worsened, as if the foul weather was slowly entering her body, the way it enters the nooks and crannies of a building. On nights the wind was right, her voice carried to the tracks that marked the border of the millsite. And as I neared the laundry I heard the sound of Wah Lee's voice as well, babbling helplessly against the current of the woman's panic. Sometimes I stopped outside the shack and considered knocking at the door, but couldn't imagine what help I might offer. Besides, I told myself, it wasn't my job to get involved.

There was heavy wind and sleet that night in February, the only time I laid eyes on her myself. I half ran, half walked along Bennet's Hill, thinking only of reaching the bunkhouses where I could get in out of the weather for fifteen minutes. The noise of the storm was deafening and my head was bowed against the rain. Mrs. Lee almost knocked me down as she ran by in a white cotton nightshirt. Her feet were bare. Her hair was loose around her head. Wah Lee came out the door of the laundry and he grabbed my arm as he went by, pulling me along as he chased after her.

She was a tiny slip of a woman, but it took both of us to cart her inside the laundry and I helped take her to the back room. "*Hala, hala,*" Wah Lee kept repeating, "*Hala.*" There was a single kerosene lamp and I could make out a small bed with an iron frame, a porcelain chamber pot on the floor that needed to be cleaned. We carried his wife to the bed, and Wah Lee fitted a leather harness that was fastened to the bed frame around her shoulders while I held her. Her nightshirt was soaked through and clung to her body. I could have counted her ribs as she strained against the harness, crying, yelling words I didn't understand. There were raw bald patches on her head where it looked like the hair had been torn from her scalp. "Prease," Wah Lee said, to me this time. "Prease." He took my arm and led me out into the laundry room where I leaned against a shelf of washed and ironed clothing. "Wife very sick," he said. "But she OK now, she OK."

"You can't keep her tied up in there like that," I said. "It's not right."

Wah Lee bobbed his head quickly. "No, no, only when wife sick. She safe here," he said. "Prease," he said.

The smell of the chamber pot and the heat of the laundry room made my stomach turn and I hurried out into the sleet, throwing up at the side of the building. Then I walked slowly toward the bunkhouses, glad for the cold rain against my face, letting it soak my head. At the bunkhouse I woke my foreman and booked off sick for the rest of the night. By morning I was running a fever so high I couldn't sit up. For three days afterwards I missed my regular shift.

I never saw Wah Lee's wife again, although I would hear her at times. Her voice from the back of the laundry was like the sound of the ocean inside an empty shell, the sickness coming and going like a tide.

It was a freak accident that ended Stick Walker's hockey career. No one can even say for sure what happened, the best guess being that a spot of blasting powder on the bit he was sharpening was ignited by sparks from the grinding stone. The steel bit exploded in his hand, shards passing through his palm, shattering bones in his wrist and arm.

By the time I made my way to the mess hall for supper that day, the news was making the rounds. No one noticed the spot of blood on his forehead until he was taken to the hospital and the much uglier wounds of the arm had been attended to. Stick reported no pain in his head, only an irritating itch around the area where the hole had been punctured. An X-ray revealed a metal splinter half an inch long sitting in the frontal lobe of the brain. There was nothing to do, the doctor concluded, but leave it there and hope for the best.

Eventually, the arm healed and he recovered almost full use of his fingers and hand. But Stick had lost his easy way, his cockiness. He was unpredictable, prone to fits of sudden rage and cursing. He couldn't stickhandle a puck or follow the flow of a game. He rarely spoke to the men in the machine shop, kept his distance at the bunkhouse. Even his closest friends before the accident became strangers to him.

He'd walk the streets at night, muttering and swearing under his breath. I'd see him approaching in the distance, drifting through the silver pools of the street lamps. And there were nights I'd come upon him standing outside the laundry, late, after Wah Lee had gone to bed. He paid no attention to me as I eased up beside him. He went on staring in through the windows, swearing quietly. "Fucking chink," he said. "Fucking chink."

I don't know why he blamed Wah Lee for the change that took place in his life rather than me. But in his mind I receded into the background, an innocent bystander in the events leading up to the accident. "Stick," I'd say quietly, placing a hand on his arm. "Stick, you'd best be getting back to the bunkhouse."

On one occasion I found him pounding with both hands on the door of the laundry. "Come out here," Stick was yelling. "You fucker, come out here!" No one stirred inside and I stood at a distance, ready to step in if I had to. After a few minutes Stick lost interest in the door and wandered off.

I should have reported him for that I suppose. I could have written him up, had him sent out of town. But even at its worst his anger had a lost, aimless feel to it, lighting on one thing for a time, then drifting elsewhere, like a moth mistaking one streetlamp after another for the moon. I never expected anything to come of it, and I'd caused him enough grief already. That was my thinking at the time.

It was late spring, the roads were bogged with mud. There was a good breeze of wind blowing across the townsite toward the mills. I heard the yelling from a long way off and tried to run, but only succeeded in falling repeatedly. By the time I reached the laundry the two men were locked in each other's arms, as if they were dancing together, drunkenly. They lurched into the oily light of a kerosene lamp on an ironing board, knocking it to the floor. I remember the sound of glass breaking, the roar of flame travelling through spilled fuel, the shelves of cleaned and pressed clothing catching fire. The light in the room flared into brightness, every corner illuminated. I tried to separate the two men, but they wouldn't let go of one another and I had to drag them through the door together. By then their clothes were burning too. They fell wrestling to the ground and I rolled them in the mud to douse the fire. "Break it up," I shouted. "Break it up."

Everything stopped when Mrs. Lee began screaming inside. The two men moved away from each other, as if a song in their heads had suddenly finished playing. Wah Lee got to his feet and moved toward the doorway, but the entire laundry was alight and he had to hold his arms up to shield his face from the heat. He shouted into the noise of the fire as it ate its way through the shack, from the inside out. I turned away then and watched Stick walk slowly toward the bunkhouse, as if he had already forgotten what had happened, why his clothes were wet with mud, why his hair smelled burnt.

While my back was turned the roof collapsed, throwing a shower of sparks at the stars.

China is ten thousand miles from Newfoundland. When I'm walking through darkness, the sun is shining there. Night and day. We used to tell kids around here that if you dug a hole from Black Rock straight through the earth you'd find yourself in the middle of China, that you'd be standing upside down. Teasing them, you see, although the literal truth of it is, if it was possible to do such a thing, that's where you'd end up.

What I think about sometimes is this: Wah Lee on the Company train in his blue pyjama suit and pig tail, not a word of English in his head, chugging toward Black Rock with that label pinned to his chest. Who addressed him like a letter and put him on that train? A little man coming alone into a place of strangers, his life turned upside down.

After the fire burned down to embers and most of the people who had come out of their houses in long underwear and boots went home, I headed down Bennett's Hill road to the bunkhouse to clock in. I was in shock, I guess. I looked up at Ellen's window as I went by, but she had given up waiting. And it occurred to me then that we were strangers, that I had no idea what it would mean to be married to her.

This was a long time ago, of course. No one remembers much about it anymore, besides myself, and I've long since given up trying to answer the old questions, though they're still with me. Was she strapped in her leather harness when the fire took her? Did she choose to stay there? Am I to blame for all of this? For a time there was nothing I wanted more than to know the answer to these things. But now I think the best I can do is simply to say as clearly as I can, "This is what happened. These are the things I saw."

There's no hint of the laundry's foundation in the ground now. The laundry tubs and ironing boards, the bed with the iron frame, the chamber pot, all of it gone, lost in the darkness. There's just myself now to say what stood here, what happened in this place. And someday soon, I know, I'll be lost in the darkness as well.

THE MEASURE

When I come to myself now I can't place the date or the hour, can't guess how long I've been out, five minutes or days on end. I know only dark or light, registering the sensations of those things from a peculiar distance, as if I've already been pulled from the current of time that runs through the world. Sometimes I think, Perhaps it's happened. Maybe this is what it means to be dead.

Mildred sitting beside the hospital bed whenever I open my eyes. She stands and leans across me, her hand on my forehead. "Hello, Maggie," she says.

Not yet, then. Not quite.

1.

When she came out of his room to the nurses' station, Mildred's face was as white as a fresh cast. "Maggie," she said, "I can't do it."

I stood up out of the chair. "What do you mean?" I said. Knowing full well what she meant.

She shook her head. "I can't."

"Jesus Christ, Midge."

"I'm sorry," she said. "I can't."

Honest to God. I don't know how she managed all these years as a nurse.

———

Art Stevenson was lying with the sheets down to his knees and the hospital nightgown pushed up over his hips. He turned his head sharply toward me when I touched him, startled. "You nurses," he said, "sneaking up on people with those fucking rubber soles." He had his top plate in a glass of water beside the bed and his toothless mouth fell in on itself like an apple dried out on a windowsill.

I said, "How about I whistle as I come in the room?" But he'd lost himself already and didn't seem to hear me. "Art," I said.

He was trying to peer past me toward the door. "What happened to that other one?" he said. He was suffering periodic seizures and had reached the point where everyone around him was a stranger, even during his brief periods of lucidity.

"What seems to be the problem here?" I asked him.

He looked up at me again and then quickly down at himself. "I can't take a piss is the problem. Help me out now would you?"

The catheter was lying on a piece of gauze beside him where Midge had left it, the tip streaked with blood.

I told him, "This is going to hurt a bit."

He only grunted and stared up at the ceiling. He was fifty-two and still a large man, although the cancer had wasted some of the bulk from his frame. His stomach was so distended by a tumour that it looked like the belly of a woman in the eighth month of a pregnancy. An exceptionally hairy woman in the eighth month of a pregnancy.

I stood beside him awhile after I was done, wiping the sweat and snot from his face as he gathered himself. "You alright now?"

He nodded. "You've got some way with that willy of mine," he said. "You wouldn't consider a little extracurricular activity once I get out of here, would you?"

I pursed my lips, as if I was giving the proposal serious thought. I was surprised by his words, by their unexpected connection to a world outside the one that had nearly swallowed him whole. He didn't know me from Eve, I could see that. But he knew he'd never leave this room alive. "You call me," I said. I touched his face and then turned off the lights on my way out of the room.

Mildred was doing charts at the nurses' station. She said, "Everything go okay?" and I gave her a look that shut her up for a few minutes.

"He shouldn't be left there like that," I said.

Midge didn't lift her eyes from the charts.

"He'd be better off," I told her.

She got up from her chair and walked to a filing cabinet. "It's not my place to say when," she said. She turned towards me. "Or how."

There was a sprain in her voice on that last word, as if she was trying to stop herself as she came down wrong on a bad ankle.

"Oh fuck off, Midge. You're worse than the doctors these days."

She shook her head.

"There's no excuse for that kind of cruelty," I said.

She went on shaking her head. She gathered up an armful of charts and headed towards the empty patient lounge.

"If it was me in there," I said to her back, trying not to shout. "By Christ," I said. "If it was me." But by then she was through the doors and out of sight.

2.

Some of what happens in this building at night you can put down to your own mind working. A persistent murmur, like voices in the empty wards or the sense you're being watched when you sit doing charts at night—you can dismiss it as a function of architecture, of too much silence, of fatigue.

Ignoring other things that go on here requires more determination. When the lights in the kitchen go on and off at night, when the television is found turned on in the empty patient lounge at four in the morning, the other nurses blame electrical surges. When all three drawers of a filing cabinet are pulled open in their absence they put it down to pranksters, ambulatory patients amusing themselves at the nurses' expense.

I prefer to accept the evidence of my own senses.

In the last decade I worked at the hospital, the doors from the wards to the nursing station would sometimes swing open of their own accord at night, as if someone was walking through. "That's The Hag now," I'd whisper, "doing her rounds."

Mildred crossed herself repeatedly, the colour draining from her face the same as if you'd taken the plug from a sink.

"For chrissakes, Midge," I'd say. "You're not even Catholic." I would pat the seat of an empty chair beside us and talk directly to the air. "Have a seat, Nurse Handrigan, we're just doing charts."

Mildred always said she wants to be cremated when she dies. She's afraid she'll wake up underground otherwise, buried alive. She'd like to believe the body is the measure of all things and that once it's taken care of she'll be safe. Gone.

3.

Midge always looked the part of a nurse, I'll grant her that. She had the breasts for it, buxom in that starched white uniform. The odd cap that looked like an oversized sailboat about to crest my forehead, she managed to set delicately at the crown like a ribbon in her thick brown hair. But the job itself never suited her. She was too much a coward, a lightning rod for panic and alarm. Even the most unlikely possibility of disaster unhinged her. During thunderstorms she hid in the broom closet beside the pharmacy, hyperventilating into a paper bag.

The first time she was called upon to insert a rectal thermometer during her training at the Grace Hospital in St. John's she fainted. Smacked her head on the metal cupboard between the beds and bled all over her uniform. We were sitting in our room, smoking and playing gin rummy on the bedspread when she confessed this to me, without so much as looking up from her hand. I stared at her. "What?" she said finally. And then she said, "It just seemed the wrong place to be putting a thermometer."

Honest to God.

For a time after I left the hospital, years later, she joined me on my daily walks to the dam with the dogs. But she couldn't make peace with their surging around her, shouting at them uselessly to settle down and clinging to my arm for fear they'd knock her over.

"I thought you liked animals," I said when she gave up the walks entirely.

She shook her head. "I like them one at a time. You can almost believe they have a soul when you deal with them one at a time."

I nodded. "They're like people that way," I told her.

When Mildred came to Black Rock, straight out of training in 1961, all the single nurses lived in the hospital residence. There were half-a-dozen rooms like the one we shared in the basement of the building: two single beds, a washstand, two small closets. I had already spent close to ten years in my tiny double room as one roommate after another married and moved out into Company houses. Most of the men employed at the mine were young and single, living in the three-story bunkhouses constructed near the Company stables, drinking heavily when they weren't on shift, fighting over the attention of the few unmarried girls in town. Like prison inmates desperate for contact with a feminine world, they fell in love quickly and repeatedly. There was something arbitrary in the whole enterprise that I found unsettling.

"You're not a bad-looking girl," Midge would tell me. "Why don't you go out?"

I had, over time, come up with a simple dismissal of the question. "I'm married to my job," I said.

"Glory hallelujah," she snorted. "No one told me I was entering the convent."

The Black Rock Miners senior hockey team was among the best in the province in those days. Every spring they endured marathon playoff series with the Corner Brook Royals and Grand Falls Cataracts and St. John's Caps in pursuit of the Herder Memorial Trophy. When the games were held at home, a handful of the players lived out of the hospital wards, having their gimpy ankles and strained knees frozen by the doctor before they limped to the rink, coming back drunk at three and four in the morning, ringing the front bell to be let in the door that was locked when visiting hours ended at nine p.m. If I was on shift I was inclined to let them stand out in the weather a good length of time before allowing them to stagger to their beds. But Mildred was naive enough to pity them their injuries and to admire their foolhardy dedication, their willingness to risk permanent injury for a boy's game. She laughed and joked with them as they came in and slapped their drunken hands away without taking real offence. She only blushed when they complained they were too stiff to remove their own pants and begged her to do it for them.

"They're just fooling around," she'd say to me when I glared. She liked attention well enough, even if she didn't care for the particular package it sometimes arrived in. When the players awoke hungover and bruised the day after a game she brought them glasses of gingerale and Aspirin, cold compresses for their shoulders or thighs, extra pillows to sit against.

Each of the players Mildred coddled through sprains and torn muscles that first year at the hospital invited her to a movie or an evening at the pool hall or to a dance. She was pretty in the way it was fashionable at the time to think of as beautiful. She had the white uniform and those formidable breasts. I used to tell her she wouldn't be single long enough to put the scent of her hair on the pillow in our little room.

4.

The animals I blame on Handrigan.

Dogs and cats always ran loose in town, roaming freely along back roads and the town limits, coming home to sleep or beg a meal of table scraps. Before the highway went through, there was no access to the veterinarian in Grand Falls. Unwanted puppies and kittens were tied in burlap bags and drowned in buckets of water. Sick dogs or cats were nursed beside wood stoves or on old blankets laid in back porches. Animals beyond hope were laid near the base of a tree or tied to a stake and shot.

People unable to stomach shooting or drowning their animals themselves, who couldn't reconcile themselves to the violence of the act even in a case where common sense seemed to demand it, had one recourse. They found their way after midnight or early in the morning before light to the service entrance of the hospital, a steel door at the end of a long corridor in the basement. They stood there knocking until Handrigan shuffled along the polished floor, her habitual contrariness magnified by the late or early hour of the day.

Handrigan was the head nurse during my first twenty years of work and I was never able to guess what motivated the woman. She had her own apartment near the nurses' residence rooms in the basement, but she had no friends to speak of and appeared to dislike her occupation as well. She resented efficiency and intelligence in her nurses and despised those who showed any sign of weakness or ineptitude. I was tolerated, but Mildred was simply a target. "Nurse Mildew," was Handrigan's name for her and she scolded and browbeat her at every opportunity.

In the privacy of our room we referred to her as *Hagrihan*, as *The Hag*. Sometimes just as *It*. Because Handrigan treated patients and staff with a cold efficiency that bordered on contempt, no one had the temerity to ask *her* why she was single, why she didn't go out. That much about her I managed to admire. I couldn't imagine the place without her, but that in itself gave no indication of how much I'd miss her once she was gone.

She had earned her reputation as the surly angel of mercy to four-legged creatures before I arrived and I never dared ask her how it came about. She would wake one of the off-duty nurses to hold a dog panting shallowly around ribs crushed by an automobile, or a cat dying of a kidney infection. She wouldn't allow the owners to accompany their animals into the hospital, unwilling to suffer the sniffling and helpless baby talk so many of them were reduced to. She stopped requesting Mildred's assistance for the same reason.

No matter the hour of an animal's arrival, there was always a distinct odour of gin on Handrigan's breath. She was never under the influence while in uniform, but she drank heavily off-duty. Except for the clandestine procedures she performed on animals, she was *unavailable* between her last round at ten p.m. and her arrival on the floor at seven-thirty the following morning.

She never spoke during the procedure except to issue instructions. She shaved a patch of fur on a front leg to find a vein and inserted the needle. She placed a hand on the neck, monitoring the pulse as it failed. When she was certain the animal had expired, she wrapped it in the sheet or blanket it arrived with and delivered it to the owners who were smoking or crying quietly or simply leaning against the cold concrete outside the steel door. She never accepted money or thanks. She took the necessary supplies from the hospital pharmacy without requesting permission or answering questions.

Handrigan always left the assisting nurse to disinfect the steel table in the basement garbage room and shuffled back to her apartment, more crooked than she'd been when the knock on the door woke her from her sleep.

5.

I wasn't a stranger to death when I left training in St. John's. I'd washed corpses still radiating the heat of life, weighted the eyelids closed, folded the arms across the chest before the body was sent to the morgue. But I had never actually watched someone die until my first year at the hospital in Black Rock, when I was twenty-four. Her name was Emma Burry, a woman not quite my age and already a mother of three. Through the nights her distress was unrelenting and she often had us take her to the patient lounge in a wheelchair where she would watch television for as long as she could remain in a sitting posture. There were just the two stations broadcasting at the time and the only thing on the air late at night was an

Indian chief test pattern, but she sat there in the grey light anyway, slumped in the wheelchair, staring up at that pale beacon as if it was guiding her through some dark passage. Her joints were filthy with cancer and there wasn't an inch of her body that didn't cause her pain. Eventually she was unable to get out of her bed at all and she suffered through the night with only the ceiling tiles for company.

I was called into the doctor's office just as I was starting an overnight shift, shortly after Emma Burry became bedridden. The doctor was pulling on his overcoat, getting ready to leave for the day. Handrigan came into the room behind me and eased the door shut. The doctor didn't look at me at first. He picked up a vial from his desk and said, "This is for Mrs. Burry." He turned to me then, his face set as if he was expecting to be called upon to defend himself. "If she asks for it," he said.

I stared at him for a moment and then at Nurse Handrigan who was standing behind me at the door. Dr. Tilley was the only physician Handrigan had worked with in Black Rock. He was an elderly man with a large white moustache that disguised his mouth and made it impossible to distinguish a smile from a frown. He never raised his voice or spoke ill of anyone. Handrigan held my eye a moment before stepping back out to the floor.

"You understand me?" Dr. Tilley said then.

I did and tried to say so, but in the end could only nod my head.

He nodded in turn, and he was smiling or frowning, it was impossible to say. "Goodnight then," he said. He went by me in his heavy coat and there was a scent of frost and spruce about him as he passed, as if his jacket had been hung outside all day.

There were six other people on the ward and Emma kept them awake most of the night, the painkillers we gave her practically useless. I stood beside her when I wasn't checking on the other patients, using a wet Q-tip to moisten her mouth, wiping the sweat from her forehead. She weighed all of eighty pounds by then, her face the colour of clipped fingernails except around the eyes where the skin was bruised black.

At five that morning she went suddenly silent. I squeezed her hand. "Mrs. Burry," I said. "Emma?"

She turned to look at me, staring out from such an unfamiliar distance that my bladder almost let go as I stood there.

"Mrs. Burry," I said again, whispering this time.

"Please," she said. She was watching me with a clarity I hadn't seen in her for weeks. "Please," she said again.

I could smell the gin on Handrigan's breath when she came to the door. "What is it?" she said angrily. The hair on one side of her head trampled down like grass an animal had slept on for a night.

"I can't," I said.

"Nurse Dawe."

"I can't. I'm sorry."

"I am not on duty," she said.

I straightened up and tried to clear the lump from my throat. I said, "I've never seen a person die."

She stared at me, coming slowly to herself. She nodded. "Alright," she said.

She wasn't in uniform when she came upstairs to the ward. She stood just inside the door of Emma's room, offering occasional instructions so quietly they seemed more like suggestions, as if she were helping a girl learn to crochet or quilt.

After I emptied the vial, I held the dying woman's hand and felt for a pulse at the wrist. Her breath ragged and uneven, then barely perceptible, then gone.

"That's it," I said. "I think that's it."

Handrigan looked at her watch. "5:27 a.m.," she said.

I nodded and looked across to the doorway where she'd been standing, but she had already left the room. Back at the nurses' station I recorded the time of death as 5:27 a.m., October 11, 1950. I stood a moment then, listening to the silence in the hospital, feeling the weight of it, as if I was submerged in water. Handrigan downstairs again and already asleep, I guessed.

In the years after we lost her, several nurses and more than one patient claimed to see Handrigan about the hospital, a blur of white out of the corner of the eye, her footfall echoing in the basement corridor. But I was the one truly haunted by her. When I stood at bedsides watching lives the like of Art Stevenson's whittled to a filament of incoherent suffering, I felt her figure behind me, out of uniform and the smell of gin on her breath. The steady murmur of her voice whispering from across the room. How completely drained of urgency it was. How nearly gentle.

6.

So. The police.

When I opened the door to Constable Anderson my first thought was, It couldn't have been Mildred. Being the coward she is.

"Ms. Dawe," he said, nodding apologetically.

It was snowing and the wind was up. I stood holding the door open with one hand, the other keeping my robe closed at my throat. The dogs were manic behind me and I used my legs to bar them inside. The knocking had woken me from a sleep so deep I felt drugged and there's no telling how long he'd been standing there hammering at the door, the dogs howling. It must have been one of the doctors, I thought.

"Sorry to wake you ma'am," he said when I made no move to let him inside. A sprinkling of snow covered his hat and the dark shoulders of his coat. It looked like a flurry of dandruff and I could just resist the urge to reach out and brush it away. "I have a few questions I have to ask you, Ms. Dawe. About the death of Art Stevenson."

I put the kettle on as the constable settled himself in the living room. Half-a-dozen dogs sniffed at his knees. Three cats lay along the back of the chesterfield behind him. His eyes darted around the room, nervous I thought. Looking for clues.

"How long since you moved out of the hospital?" he called to me in the kitchen.

I walked back to the living room before answering. "They closed up the residence beds fifteen years ago now. Needed the space for storage, they said."

"Do you miss it?"

I looked at him and shrugged. "A blessing in disguise probably. I'd never have been able to take in the animals if I didn't buy this place for myself. I was the only one still living in the hospital by then anyway. I was in Nurse Handrigan's old apartment."

"The Hag?" he said.

I smiled at him. "I'm surprised you remember her."

"Mostly before my time, actually. I've heard stories enough though."

I nodded again and looked down at my feet. It was Mildred who found her, lying in bed in her uniform, the bottle of gin on the floor beside her. The empty bottle of pills on the nightstand. The doctor cited *heart failure* as the cause of death to spare her the formal investigation, the autopsy.

The constable ran a hand through his carefully combed hair.

"It seems like only yesterday," I said, "that I delivered you."

He smiled uncomfortably.

"You gave us quite the time that night, coming out feet first the way you did. For a while there I was afraid I was going to lose you both."

"Yes, ma'am," he said. "I've heard all about that."

"Your mother said she was afraid you'd end up doing things backward your whole life and now look at you."

He nodded again. "I have a few things I need to clear up," he said. He took a notebook from his breast pocket and opened it on his knee. "There have been some questions raised about Art Stevenson's death, Ms. Dawe. I understand you were on shift last night when it occurred?"

I nodded and reached to touch the back of my head, a knot of pain starting to pulse there.

"You recorded the time of death, is that correct?"

"Yes, that's correct."

He nodded at the page where he made notes with a stub of pencil. "Ms. Dawe, was Mr. Stevenson alive when you entered his room last night at around 3:15 a.m.?"

I cleared my throat. "You could call it that, I suppose. The machines said he was still alive. If that's how you measure such things."

"And he died in your presence, is that correct?"

My head hurt so much it was difficult to see, to focus my eyes.

"Ms. Dawe?" he said, waiting. "Ms. Dawe, we are going to require answers to these questions."

"Excuse me," I said, getting up to see to the kettle.

The constable followed me into the kitchen. "Ms. Dawe, did you give Mr. Stevenson an injection of morphine last night around 3:15 a.m.?"

I turned from the counter holding two mugs. "Milk or sugar?" I asked.

7.

Mildred became engaged to one of her hockey players within a year of her arrival at the hospital. Sherm Mackey wasn't the most offensive of the bunch, at least, I gave her credit for that. But I resented the marriage. It was so obvious a thing, so predictable. As if Midge was surrendering to a predetermined life without a murmur of protest. When she asked me to stand as her maid of honour I said no, as a kind of protest, a refusal to be complicit in what I thought of as her acquiescence. "Are you my friend or not?" she asked me. Tears welling up in her eyes.

"Goddamn it, Midge," I said, angrily, trying to disguise the surge of helplessness I felt.

After the reception cold plate, the chairs and tables were cleared back to the walls and the wedding party joined the new couple for the first dance of the evening. The best man was one of Sherman's hockey buddies. He bowed slightly before the music began. "Maid of honour," he said. He was already drunk and I kept as much distance between us as a waltz allowed. He said, "You are a lovely thing." I bit my lip and kept my eyes averted. He said, "You wouldn't consider a little extracurricular activity when this shindig is over, would you?" He slipped his hand down the small of my back.

"Art Stevenson," I said, "you leave that hand where it is or I swear to Jesus you'll never hold a hockey stick again."

When the dance ended I walked past the bride and hissed at her: "You owe me one, Midge."

She turned her face to me, her pretty smile vacant, confused. "What do you mean?"

"You *owe* me," I said again.

After she and Sherman moved out into their company house, Mildred had five children in succession with hardly a month's breathing space between pregnancies.

"For chrissakes," I said to her after the fourth, "you're not even Catholic! Make him wear a rubber."

She shrugged helplessly. "He doesn't like them." And when I glared she straightened her shoulders. She said, "I love children."

"Well and it serves you right then," I said.

———————

Handrigan used to say, "If you X-rayed Mildred's head you'd find her arsehole."

I disliked her for those words, for the frequency and the casual sincerity with which they were spoken. I disliked her for the fact that I found myself thinking them so often myself. It was as if I was the Head Nurse's successor in more than hospital hierarchy, that I was a Handrigan-in-waiting and merely had to become more myself to have her surface in all her obstinate, pig-headed glory. *Mildred is your friend*, I told myself to choke back those words. *She is a decent person. She is not a bad nurse.* All but the last of which was true enough.

Except for the occasional shift covering for a sick nurse, Midge was away from the hospital most of ten years, until her youngest started school. Shortly after coming back to a regular position, she found Handrigan lying dead in her room.

"Poor soul," Mildred kept repeating, sitting in the lunchroom where I was making her a cup of tea.

"She's probably better off," I said.

There had been rumours that the hospital administration was about to force Handrigan out of her job. It wasn't until we sifted through her papers and documents that we discovered she was almost seventy and had been fighting mandatory retirement for years.

Handrigan had no surviving family we knew of and I was assigned the task of writing her obituary, having worked with her longer than anyone else at the hospital. I sat with Midge at her kitchen table on a Saturday afternoon, a school exercise book open in front of us.

"Passed away peacefully," Midge said aloud as she wrote carefully along the lined page.

"Peacefully! Jesus, Midge."

She started over. "Passed away unexpectedly." She trapped the tip of her tongue between her bottom lip and her teeth as she pressed the words into the paper. Her husband came into the kitchen behind us to make himself another drink. Mildred said, "Leaving to mourn . . . "

There was a pause.

She looked up at me. "There's us," she said.

"Yes," I said. "And the makers of Beefeater Gin."

Sherm laughed over his tray of ice cubes. "And the Central Newfoundland Bachelors Club," he said.

"You *friggers.*"

"Now Mildred," I said.

"I'll do this myself," she said. She was fighting tears as she closed the exercise book and walked off into the living room.

Sherm leaned against the counter with his drink and let out a long breath of air. "Things won't be the same without her, I imagine," he said.

Mildred was against me taking over Handrigan's apartment, though she never said so in any but the most indirect ways. "How can you sleep in that bed?" she asked me.

I thought of the times I'd seen her pregnant, with an infant in her arms and another hanging off her clothes, when I thought to ask her the same question.

"How *can* you?" she insisted.

I bit my tongue. But I knew what she was worried about and felt it too: that I would wind up living down there on my own, getting through my nights with a limitless prescription of gin. The path from the bed to the bathroom, from the bed to the cupboard in the kitchenette where Handrigan kept her bottle, were worn into the tiles like walking trails beaten through meadow grass.

The minister at Handrigan's funeral was new to Black Rock and a stranger to us all. "A life has its own internal logic," he said from the pulpit. He was a young man, the minister, a red-haired boy from the mainland working in his first parish. "We are born to die, our bodies inscribed with our mortality. With our sister Doris Handrigan the Lord has been merciful. Three score years and ten, she knew the full measure of our life on this earth."

Amen, I heard someone whisper behind me.

8.

Mildred was on shift when I was carried into the hospital that February evening. She moved about the bed with an uncharacteristic energy and efficiency, cutting away my clothes, setting up an IV, while the other nurse tried to reach the doctor at home.

I was barely conscious, exhausted, half-frozen. "The animals," I said. "Who's going to feed the animals?"

"Those goddamn dogs," Midge said. "An old woman out there alone with those savages. I knew they were going to knock you over sooner or later."

"It wasn't the dogs," I lied to her. "I just fell on the ice."

"Shut up now," she said, still cutting away fabric. "Don't try to speak."

In the years after Art Stevenson died, I'd lived off my savings and the small pension the hospital administration were too cowardly to withhold when they forced me out of my job. Without nursing, all I had to get up for were the animals I started taking in when I moved out of Handrigan's apartment: strays, three-legged dogs, blind cats that would have ended up in the woods with a bullet in their skulls otherwise. People left unwanted puppies and kittens at my door, foundlings in cardboard boxes. I walked the gravel road to the dam every day, summer and winter, knee-deep in a current of mutts. I operated a pet grooming service in the basement of my house, though the business consisted mostly of work on my own menagerie of hand-me-downs.

After I left, the hospital became something closer to a chronic care facility than a working hospital, winding down as the shafts were mined out and closed and young people moved on to jobs elsewhere. The population of Black Rock fell to half its size in less than a decade, then to a third. Hospital staff was cut to seven nurses and a single doctor, the lab and X-ray departments were closed. The few beds in use were most often occupied by retired miners whose lungs had been ruined underground, by pensioners waiting to die.

Mildred came into her own with the older folks, with the widowers, with the grandmothers whose only relatives lived in other towns, other provinces, other countries. She could talk the ear off a fence post given the chance, and she was endlessly patient, listening to stories repeated endlessly if required. She never forgot a birthday or anniversary, handing out homemade cards, baking cookies for those who could still eat them.

"You always were more of a nursemaid than a nurse," I told her. "You're welcome to that, as far as I'm concerned."

Mildred nodded, knowing I didn't mean a word of it.

We saw each other on her off days and on weekends. We volunteered together with the Red Cross at the monthly blood donor clinics in the Legion Hall. Mildred told me the joke around town was not to let Maggie Dawe near you with the needle or you'd never get out of the Legion alive.

You had to laugh.

Midge and I laughed a lot, which is what got us through the rough spots. She could have ended the whole affair at the start, she could have told them she was with me when Art Stevenson died. They wouldn't have been able to push me out if Mildred had stood up to them. But Midge couldn't face the truth when she should have, and couldn't deny the truth when the situation demanded it. She always was a coward. Knowing that made it a little easier to forgive her. If you measure a friendship only by its failures, I decided, you wind up living alone.

Before I became too ill to talk at all, our conversations inevitably came back to the dogs, to my foolhardiness, my stubborn stupidity. "What would have become of you out there if the constable hadn't come along on his rounds?" she wanted to know.

I turned away from her to look out the window. How long had I been lying there before he came by? The dogs whining and running off and coming back to lick at my face. Two or three lying beside me on the icy road, although I stopped feeling anything like heat from their bodies long before it got dark.

"You'd have frozen to death out there, that's what would have happened."

"I'd have been better off," I wheezed.

Midge pointed a finger. "Don't you start with that," she said. "I won't hear it."

I made a motion with my head, to say I knew what she would or wouldn't hear. "What about the animals?" I asked her again.

She said, "Sherm is taking care of the animals."

I stared a moment. "I'll bet he loves that," I said.

Mildred smiled at me. "If he knows what's good for him," she said, "he'll pretend he does."

The multiple fractures of my hip and pelvis required the insertion of pins to heal in any sensible way, but pneumonia set in shortly after I was admitted which made surgery impossible. I drifted in and out of consciousness as the illness surged and faded, my mind clouded by the medication that dripped into my arm. Whenever I opened my eyes Mildred was beside the bed.

She leaned across me, her hand on my forehead. "Hello, Maggie," she said. She washed my face and neck with a warm cloth, she rubbed my feet with liniment, the medicinal scent of it coming to me through what felt like layers of gauze between my senses and the world. She carried on an endless monologue, telling me about the weather, about her children living in St. John's or Fort McMurray. She talked about me getting well, about the walks to the dam we had ahead of us.

Occasionally I was well enough to say different. I would squeeze her hand, shaking my head. "I'm seventy-four years old," I told her. "I'll never get out of here alive."

"Shhh," she said. "Shhh. Don't try to speak."

When I began throwing up the hospital food, she brought soup she'd cooked at home, leaning in over the bed to spoon-feed it to me. Eventually I couldn't even keep that down and she stood there holding the bowl helplessly while it went cold in her hand. It was painful to watch her watch me dying. She stroked my face, asking if there was anything I needed, if there was anything she could do for me.

I looked at her then, to say she knew what I wanted. "Are you my friend or not?" I whispered. The words so heavy with the fluid in my lungs they could have been wrung out like sponges.

She shook her head.

"You owe me this much," I told her. "You owe me."

Something unfamiliar in her face then, something hard. Immovable. "I will not," she said. "Do you hear me? I *won't*."

What a time, I thought, for a woman to find a backbone.

9.

It will probably fall to Mildred to write my obituary and I can imagine how it will read—the prevarication, the well-meaning lies. If it was left to me, I'd put it this way: *After a brief illness, Maggie Dawe (1925–1999), pensioner, animal lover, subject of inconclusive police investigations, defrocked nurse, Red Cross volunteer, petulant patient. Survived by eleven dogs of varying pedigree, by eight sullen cats. Leaving to mourn Mildred Mackey, R.N., senior staff person and head nurse of Handrigan Memorial Hospital.*

Maybe I'll push my way through the swinging doors when she works the night shift, to let her know I'm still around, to say I'm still here.

That I forgive her.

She'll cross herself when she looks up from her work, though only once, forehead, breastbone, right shoulder, then the left, and slowly, slowly, the way a person might touch someone they love. The way she touched me at the end, that gentle refusal. Just the slightest hint of a smile on her face.

"That's only Maggie," she'll say to the nurse on duty with her. "On her rounds."

And I'll take my place in the empty chair beside them.

CELESTIALS

He's sitting under the green plastic awning of the restaurant near his school. The heat is oppressive. Even the exertion required to eat leaves Patrick dripping in sweat. His head aches.

She Ze Ming sits across from him in a white cotton shirt, the sleeves rolled to his elbows. His dark hair, parted on the side, is streaked with grey. There are small lines of perspiration at his temples.

Patrick picks up his napkin to wipe the sweat from his forehead. "I wonder how hot it is," he says aloud, though mostly to himself.

"It is thirty-eight degrees of course," Ming announces with a note of mock surprise, and he smiles that peculiar smile of his, mischief coupled with something like fatalism. For the first time, his smugness irritates Patrick.

"There is a law in China," Ming continues in his formal but impeccable English. "If the temperature rises above thirty-eight, the factories are required to send their workers home." He smiles again. "If you understood enough to listen to the radio or the television, you would know the temperature never rises above thirty-eight degrees in Hefei."

Ming had spent a year in Canada, working for a small technical firm that had embarked on a number of "joint ventures" with western companies. He was a cynical man, Patrick thought, but generally good-natured, and his knowledge of the peculiarities of life in China, and his willingness to share that knowledge with a westerner, had made him a valuable acquaintance.

"You are from Newfoundland?" he said to Patrick when they first met. "Then we are compatriots, I believe. We are both children of third world countries."

This was in February, during the Spring Festival. The schools were closed for the month and most of the other foreign teachers at Patrick's university had left the city to travel. They were both guests at the home of Mr. Shu, an English teacher at Ke Da. In the unheated apartment they sat around the table in wool sweaters and bulky down jackets.

"You've been to Newfoundland?" Patrick said to Ming, not sure how to take his comment.

"No, I am sorry, I have not. I have been to Toronto."

"You will excuse She Ze Ming," Mr. Shu interrupted. "He has, as you say, had one too many."

"A toast," Ming said, raising his cup, ignoring his host, "to Mr. Patrick. I understand Mr. Patrick, that 'Newfies,' if you will permit me, are great drinkers? Is this not so?"

Patrick raised his glass cautiously. "Compared to Torontonians," he said, "yes, we are great drinkers."

"Aha!" Ming shouted. "*Gan-bai*," he said.

"Ganbay," Patrick replied.

Patrick's hometown in Newfoundland was a community of less than three thousand. There were two schools (public and Catholic), a post office, a hockey rink, an outdoor tennis court where a piece of wire fencing served as the net on the third court, a zinc mine and milling operation that was about to close permanently, and one restaurant that doubled as a teen hangout officially called The Garden Restaurant, but known to everyone as "Wong's."

Wong lived in an apartment above the restaurant, and from what Patrick could tell, had no life outside his work. He acted as waiter, cashier, cook, dish-washer, and if the need arose, bouncer, a role in which he was surprisingly quite effective. It wasn't his physical size that made people wary of him. He was a tall thin man, and Patrick's friends often joked that his slim waist was evidence that even Wong couldn't stomach his own food. It was his *strangeness* that intimidated people, his Chinese epithets, the way his eyes widened behind the thick lenses of his black-rimmed glasses. Who could say what he was capable of? His white apron was stained with grease and gravy, with red splotches of sweet and sour sauce. His dark hair was cut short and stood straight up from his scalp.

At the front of the restaurant there were two pinball machines and the town's young people took this as a direct invitation, though the benefits of the arrangement to Wong were not apparent to Patrick. He and his friends rarely spent money there beyond an occasional can of Coke, or a few quarters for pinball. On the rare occasions they did order food, it was fairly standard practice when the dishes arrived to inform the waiter he had erred in taking their orders: "No, no, no, not chicken balls. You got it wong! This is wong!"

He had learned to ignore them for the most part, but every evening brought confrontations of some sort. Wong yelled at them if someone tilted the pinball machine too vigorously, coming out from behind the counter to stare ominously. Once or twice each night, he cleared the restaurant after some incident or other, a fight breaking out or a bottle being smashed on the floor. The young people would sit on the concrete steps in front of the restaurant for half an hour, then slowly begin drifting inside again. This elaborate ritual was repeated almost every night of Patrick's adolescence, and both parties seemed to have accepted it and their allotted roles, for reasons that probably neither could have explained.

Patrick became a regular guest at She Ze Ming's home after the Spring Festival.

Ming's wife, Lou Do, was a cheerful woman who smiled at Patrick a great deal, nodding her head and shaking his hand with both hands when he arrived and departed. Her dark face seemed to Patrick to be perpetually tired, which gave her cheerfulness a sense of dignity, made it seem almost heroic to him. Her hair was completely grey though she couldn't have been more than forty. She continually refilled his plate, bringing more and more food to the table and indicating with her gestures that he was to eat more, drink more. Patrick wished he could talk with her, but she spoke no English and Ming seemed frustrated with translating anything more than brief exchanges. As if to compensate for his wife's inadequacy, Ming always invited friends or co-workers to engage in conversation with his foreign acquaintance.

"I became quite interested in your home while I lived in Toronto, Mr. Patrick, in its history," She Ze Ming told him on the evening that Lou Ning joined them for the first time. "Life there was very harsh, I understand, until you became part of

Canada. Though I must be honest, no one in Toronto seemed to know very much about it. It reminded me a great deal of how we Mandarin people know next to nothing about the minorities of the north. We assume they are dirty and stupid and lucky to be part of our great country."

"She Ze Ming!" Lou Ning said, reproaching him. It was almost the first thing she had said the entire evening. She was a young woman Patrick guessed from her appearance, not yet thirty, a co-worker of Ming's.

"You disagree?" Patrick asked her.

Lou Ning stared into her bowl and shook her head.

"Lou Ning is a great patriot, Mr. Patrick," Ming informed him. "She will not abide any criticism of her country or her people." He smiled at her, not altogether kindly Patrick thought.

Ming's wife was busy clearing dishes from the table. Patrick offered to assist her, although he knew it was useless.

"Sit down, sit down," Ming ordered him. "In China, the guest does not help. It makes the host nervous." He smiled as he took out a cigarette and lit it.

"She Ze Ming," Lou Ning said, still staring at the space on the table where her bowl had been sitting, "as host, are you not to help your wife?" There was a slight smile on her face. She was a very beautiful woman, Patrick thought. Her dark, straight hair was cropped short at the neck, her lips were fuller and her complexion lighter than most Chinese people Patrick had seen.

"Lou Ning would like to travel to the United States or Canada to work with one of our groups," Ming told Patrick, ignoring her question. "I think she will have to improve her

English very much before she is chosen. Perhaps you would be able to offer her some assistance?"

Patrick looked at her. He wasn't sure if she understood what had been said or not. "I would be happy," he said to her, speaking slowly, "to offer tutorial lessons in English if you are interested."

Ning smiled without showing her teeth. She nodded.

She Ze Ming accompanied Patrick to Lou Ning's apartment on the evening of the first tutorial. They rode their bicycles off the main streets and through a maze of small unlighted laneways. They crossed a small bridge and on the left a large field opened up. Patrick could smell manure, compost, running water. They turned right, up another narrow laneway on the other side of the field, the bell of a bike coming towards them in the darkness like a buoy warning of shallow water or rocks.

"Here," Ming announced finally.

"I'll never find this place on my own," Patrick told him.

"Well," Ming said as he locked his bike in front of the apartment building, "perhaps we can arrange to have Lou Ning come to your apartment at Ke Da after tonight."

"I'm not sure her husband would approve of that," Patrick said carelessly, meaning it as a joke.

Ming stopped and looked at Patrick. "Lou Ning lives with her parents here. She and her husband are divorced." He turned away and started up the stairs before Patrick could reply. "It is quite unusual in China," he went on. "To divorce, I mean. It is legal of course, but it is not accepted. There is still a sense of shame attached to it here. Her husband was

. . . very unkind, shall we say. But it is Lou Ning who is blamed for leaving, by most people. She has a daughter who lives here as well."

Lou Ning met them at the door and invited them in, introducing both Patrick and She Ze Ming to her parents. Ning's father and mother nodded and spoke a few words to Ming. To Patrick's eyes they both seemed a little guarded. Ming assured him this caution was common among the older generation when they first met foreigners. They were both dressed in non-descript blues and greys, the uniform of the proletariat.

They sat together at a dark wooden table in the front room, drinking Chinese green tea and eating sunflower seeds. As they talked, Ning's parents cracked the shells in their mouths, scooping the tiny seed with their tongue and spitting the shells onto the floor. Both Ming and Ning were more discreet, spitting the shells into bowls.

Ning's daughter stood at her mother's side, alternately staring at, and deliberately ignoring, Patrick. Ning tried to convince her to say "hello" in English, but her daughter simply buried her face in Ning's dress and shook her head furiously. Her grandparents found this both unacceptable and hilarious. The grandfather shouted at her in Chinese while he laughed, coaxing her. Ning bent to kiss the top of her daughter's head, her hands at the sides of the girl's face to hold her still. Patrick felt he had never seen such an expression of tenderness between two people.

That evening, surrounded by Ning's family in the dull yellow glow of the overhead light, Patrick felt as if he had no past. Everything he'd experienced to this point in his life seemed small and meaningless. He felt privileged and honoured to have found his way into the home of such people, to be welcomed by them.

When he left that evening, little had been done in the way of English tutoring, beyond arranging for Lou Ning to meet him at his apartment in the Foreign Guest House the following week. But Patrick had decided that he might possibly be falling in love with his new student.

During his undergraduate degree in university, Patrick took a course in Newfoundland history. Over twelve weeks the Europeans arrived, suffered through scurvy and tuberculosis, established the fishery, exterminated the indigenous Beothuk, fought over territory, collapsed into national bankruptcy and a British Commission of Government, and voted narrowly to join Canada.

The first small group of Asians arrived in St. John's during the nineteenth century, having been refused entry into Canada. Local papers referred to them as "celestials" and described, in some detail, their clothes, features and manners. They were all men—immigration laws throughout North America forbade Chinese women from emigrating to prevent permanent settlement. It wasn't until 1949 that the legislation disallowing entry of women and children into Newfoundland was abolished. By that time, more than two hundred Chinese men lived on the island, the majority in St. John's, others scattered in more remote communities. There are still, his professor told the class, one or two surviving locations of the Chinese laundries which were established in St. John's at the beginning of this century.

The ping pong room in the basement of Patrick's residence had been painted by a pair of Chinese students who lived in Bowater House a few years before Patrick arrived and was known to everyone as "The Golden Rooster." The walls were gold and dark scarlet, with illustrations of dragons and fighting cocks. The two Chinese students had been the university's undisputed table tennis champions, and they were popular with the other house members because of it. They were brought to parties and sports events, like mascots.

Patrick often wondered how they ended up in Newfoundland and what had become of them. No one seemed to remember what their real names were. Most people had referred to them as Ping and Pong, often speaking of them as a unit. *Where's Ping Pong? Has anyone seen Ping Pong?*

Patrick's weekly tutorial sessions with Lou Ning began at seven p.m. She arrived with She Ze Ming, who had offered to accompany her from her parents' home to the university. Patrick would pour Chinese tea as they exchanged pleasantries. After a few minutes of conversation, She Ze Ming would excuse himself. He sat in the kitchen while the tutorial was conducted in the living room.

Patrick and Lou Ning sat facing each other in scarlet velvet-covered arm chairs. Lou Ning rarely made eye contact. Under the pretext of improving her conversational skills, Patrick would ask her to speak about herself, her job, her daughter, her own childhood, what she knew about Canada.

Her husband and her marriage were never mentioned. Patrick couldn't say why, but he was utterly charmed by the woman's reticence, her self-effacement. At times she reminded him of the traditional Chinese drawings he'd seen, black ink sketches created with a single brush stroke. She had the same simplicity and stillness of form, the same beautiful fragility.

At times he was so completely engrossed in looking at her, in watching her mouth as she spoke, or her ringless fingers on the arms of the chair, that he would find himself startled by a lull. Inevitably, he would ask the first question that came to mind, one that rarely had anything to do with the conversation which preceded it. This never failed to make Lou Ning blush, and grow even more still in her chair.

"Do you think that women are treated equally in China?" was one of his more regrettable blunders. As soon as he'd said it, he thought of her husband.

Lou Ning considered the matter seriously for a moment. "Mao," she began, "has said that women are as important to our country as men, that the revolution has freed us. Women can hold up half of heaven, he said." And she smiled then, with her mouth closed, so that Patrick could not tell if she meant to agree with Mao or refute him.

After an hour or so had passed, She Ze Ming's noisy shuffling in the next room would indicate that the tutorial should be wrapped up. Patrick and Lou Ning would move to the kitchen where he would try unsuccessfully to convince his guests to stay for more tea.

"We could not impose," She Ze Ming would explain, despite Patrick's insistence that it was still quite early. Patrick would accompany them downstairs to their bicycles where

Lou Ning would shake his hand and thank him for his assistance. He would present her with a small gift, candy or a hair buckle, for her daughter. Ning would refuse in a helplessly extravagant fashion before aquiescing, and then she and Ming would ride off together toward the university gate.

"If you do get the opportunity to go to North America," Patrick asked Lou Ning one evening, "would you consider staying there?" He had been caught staring again. If he were being brutally honest with himself, Patrick would have to admit that this statement was the closest he had ever come to broaching the subject of marriage.

Nothing had happened between the two that suggested Lou Ning was even considering Patrick in a romantic light, but his own sense of arrival, of having stumbled on something important and irrefutable, convinced him it was possible, even inevitable. Lou Ning stared at him with a surprised look on her face, and for one awful, hopeful moment Patrick thought she had some idea of what lay behind his question. But she simply shook her head. "It is not permitted," she said. "We have an obligation to our country."

Patrick heard She Ze Ming coughing loudly down the short hallway. On very rare occasions, Ming had interrupted from the kitchen to voice his opinion on the subject of their conversation. From where he was sitting, Patrick could see Ming's crossed legs at the table, the blue cloud of smoke from his cigarette.

"Our patriot," Ming announced loudly, "neglects to tell you that our government rarely allows those of us who work abroad to travel with our families. To ensure that we do return to fulfil our 'obligations.'"

Ning turned her head away from Patrick as Ming spoke, and Patrick kept his eyes down as well. He was embarrassed for her and angry at Ming's callousness. He thought of the unnamed cruelty she had suffered in her life, and he felt a sudden urge to cradle her like a child.

"Tell me," Ning said to break the silence. "Why have you come to China?"

During the summer before Patrick's last undergraduate year at university, Wong bought the building next to his restaurant, an old hardware store that had recently gone out of business. He refurbished it and opened a grocery store. Wong continued to operate the restaurant and the store was staffed by his wife, a small woman whose black hair was perpetually tied back in a bun. She had arrived only a year or two before and spoke very little English at the time. She wore a constant, uncertain smile as an apology for her linguistic shortcomings. It caused a bit of a stir, Patrick remembered, when people realized there might be more to Wong than the restaurant, the hours in the kitchen, the endless arguments with intoxicated teenagers. Everyone called his wife Mrs. Wong, though Patrick learned much later that she would have kept her own name when she married.

Patrick, Bill Murphy and Fraser Sharpe walked by the new store late one night after the bar at the Union Hall had closed. There were posters of daily specials in the large front window, a *Closed* sign in the door. "And look at this fucking place," Fraser shouted, the way a man will shout at a flat tire or an engine he can't fix. They had spent most of the evening drinking, and discussing what they would be doing a year from now when they finished university. Fraser was talking about moving to the mainland to look for work; both Bill and Patrick were considering grad school.

Bill stood in front of the store window and began grunting the spastic bass-line of The Knack's "My Sharona," then burst into song: "Dollar fifty-nine a pound, Wong's bologna!" He was playing an air guitar furiously. Fraser looked up at the windows of the apartment over the restaurant. "Hey," he shouted. "Hey, not chicken balls! You got it wong, man! This is wong!"

When he managed to stop laughing long enough to speak, Patrick told them to shut up. "They're asleep up there," he said.

"I'll bet they're not asleep," Fraser said. "I'll bet they're fucking up there. Making babies. Wong's probably working on his dynasty, the horny bastard."

"He's probably going to buy out the Company next," Bill said. "Needs workers for the mill, that's what he's doing up there."

"Fuck," Fraser said. "Fucking Chinks." And he bent over for a rock and threw it through the plate glass window at the front of the store.

Patrick doesn't remember much after that. He remembers running and falling, and then running again. And he remembers, just as he started past the restaurant, a light coming on in the apartment above it.

They sat together in the thirty-eight degree heat, under the green awning of the restaurant near Patrick's school. His head ached, a knot of anxiety knuckled his stomach. Patrick had invited Ming here to speak about something, but so far had been unable to, even though his anger had grown steadily throughout the meal.

He'd forgotten, after his most recent tutorial session, to give Ning her daughter's present, a child's spelling book. He found it on the table by the door after seeing them off downstairs, and he decided to try and catch them on his bicycle. Patrick caught sight of the two of them across the open field. He was too out of breath to call. As he pedalled to catch up, they suddenly turned left, instead of right up the laneway to Ning's apartment. At first he didn't understand where they were going and continued after them.

They bicycled down a main street toward a large city park, stopped to lock their bikes at a metal rack nearby, then walked into the trees. It was just after dusk. As they moved behind a stand of shrubs, Patrick could see them talking quietly together. Ming placed his hand on Ning's shoulder and she touched his face, with the same tenderness, Patrick thought, that he had seen when she kissed her daughter the evening he first visited her apartment.

Ming had told him about this sort of thing when they first met. The lack of housing space in many Chinese cities meant that couples often shared a bedroom with siblings or parents. During the warm weather the parks were publicly accepted as a place for "consummation." He thought about their insistence on leaving each evening as soon as the tutorial was completed, the deferential suspicion of Lou Ning's parents when they first met She Ze Ming. It was like watching a movie a second time, after dozing through the first showing.

Patrick scooped a little rice into his mouth, then placed his bowl on the table, resting the chopsticks across the top. Ming sensed his animosity as it grew, and he became increasingly less cheerful himself, lapsing into longer and longer silences.

Patrick lifted his glass of beer to rinse his mouth. "I know about you and Lou Ning," he said finally.

Ming's face settled into an impassive, almost expressionless mask.

Patrick looked across the table at his friend. "You're a married man, She Ze Ming," he said. As if it was someone else's hurt he was concerned with.

Ming smiled at Patrick without humour. "There is much you do not understand about our country," he said, in a low voice. "If I thought it was possible to leave my wife, I would not have returned from Canada. I am an intellectual, Patrick. My wife and I—my *first* wife and I—taught at a university before the Cultural Revolution. We had many friends there, colleagues. We had a son. I was one of the lucky ones, they did not kill me at least. They sent me to the countryside to be 're-educated,' to work with the peasants. I was there seven years altogether. I thought I would die there."

Ming picked up Patrick's glass and filled it with beer, then filled his own. The beer was warm and didn't pour well, and the froth ran down the sides of the glasses.

"That is where I met Lou Do and married her. It was a practical decision you understand. For both of us. It was a harsh life, a difficult life to survive on your own." Ming stopped for a moment, sitting with both his hands resting on the table. "She has no schooling, nothing," he said. "She would be sent back to that if I left her."

Patrick looked away from Ming. He felt disoriented and panicky, like a man lost in a forest and travelling in circles. "And what about Lou Ning," he said. "How can you do this to her?"

Ming's eyes widened with surprise, almost amusement. "Lou Ning is not a child," he said. "She does not need your protection Patrick, nor mine. We have found ourselves in a situation we can do little about. We have decided to make do, as best we can. I am sorry if that disappoints you."

The weather had cooled a little by the time Patrick left the country in September. But there were still days when the temperature climbed above thirty, like the afternoon he sat in the terminal at the airport in Beijing, waiting for his flight. He was alone at a table on the upper level with a beer, tracing letters into the condensation on the outside of the glass. There was a small radio over the bar playing mostly American hits from the '70s: the Jackson Five, John Denver, Creedence Clearwater Revival, The Cars.

He'd had the option of staying for another year of teaching, but decided against it. She Ze Ming, his wife, and Lou Ning had seen him off at the train station in Hefei, although he hadn't spent a great deal of time with any of them in the six weeks before he left, and the tutorial sessions had ended after the lunch at the restaurant. He'd watched them standing on the platform as the train pulled out. It seemed strange to him that they didn't look unhappy together. Lou Do rested a hand in the crook of Ning's arm and waved with the other.

A vaguely familiar tune on the radio caught his attention, the tinny thump of the guitar like background static at first. He cocked his head, listening, but couldn't quite identify the song until the muscular vocals of the chorus kicked in. *My, my, my, my, my Sharona.*

It was an eighteen hour flight back to Newfoundland and the thought of it exhausted him. Such a long way to have come, a year on the other side of the world. But in almost every way that mattered he had never managed to leave.

DIASPORA

Before she'd turned fifteen, Karen had already made up her mind she would never fall in love or marry. It was too precocious a vow to make publicly, but she honoured it in private with an unwavering, almost religious, rigour. Through her teens, she avoided any brush with romance, however slight. She even attended her high school graduation alone and danced only once, during the student/parent waltz.

"It's like dancing with a goddamn rake," her father announced afterwards, within her hearing. "That girl has more ribs than a schooner." Her mother patted her hand and assured her she looked beautiful. As far as Karen was concerned, she had stopped caring either way.

"If love was a foreign country," she wrote to Ingrid in Finland, "it would be last on my list to see."

By the time she began her first year of junior high, Karen had pen pals in eleven different countries. She spent an hour of each weekday evening writing letters about her school, typical weather in central Newfoundland, the Royal Canadian Mounted Police. She spent her five dollars a week allowance exclusively on overseas postage. It meant that she saw a lot of Mr. Varley, the post master, a portly man in his thirties, a carefully clipped mustache and a jowled, unsmiling face. His expression was as constant as the portrait of the Queen on postage stamps.

Karen liked to imagine that she was Mr. Varley's daughter, rather than her father's, despite the fact that he greeted her with a nod that was professional, just short of dismissive. "A book of ten stamps, please," Karen asked, as politely as she imagined asking him to pass the salt at the supper table. "One for Tanzania, one for Hong Kong and one for Australia." She was sure no one else in the entire town requested postage for Tanzania and it frustrated her that he was so persistently disinterested, consulting the list of rates as if he were looking up a telephone number for a stranger, passing her the stamps without a word. He looked past her to the next customer before she had pocketed her change. He was married with children of his own, she knew, and she doubted if her mother even talked to him anymore. But she couldn't help imagining, just the same.

She dropped her letters into the mail slot, standing on tiptoe to follow their slide into the grey mail bag. She thought of the scatter of destinations they were headed for, all those other lives she hadn't wound up living. On the wall of her bedroom she'd Scotch taped a map of the world and she used coloured pins to mark the countries where her pen pals lived. "My glory," her mother said, examining the pins that had gone up since her last inspection, "I never heard of half these places."

Karen's obsession with letter writing disturbed her mother. It seemed she was simply watching life happen, like someone addicted to a soap opera. And the truth was, Karen sometimes felt the loneliness her mother's concern implied. In her Grade 9 history class, they'd studied the African diaspora in the Carribean and the Americas, the Irish diaspora in the wake of the Great Irish Potato Famine. It was a word that came to mind when she thought of the places her letters were sent, her thoughts and confessions and what she could muster of affection sealed and mailed away to Brazil, Iceland, Tokyo, Burundi. At times she felt there were pieces of herself living everywhere on the planet but *here*.

Karen looked up at the map her mother was studying, at the bright fan of coloured pins. "I'm going to visit them all someday," she said.

Her mother paused for a moment. She was thinking how ridiculous an idea this was, how it couldn't help but lead to disappointment, and she considered saying something to that effect. But in the end all she said was, "Now don't be greedy."

On an afternoon in November Karen purchased stamps for Taiwan at Ted's wicket in the downtown post office. After their first brief encounter he began treating her like a long-lost relative, shouting a greeting whenever she walked into the post office, timing his work with other customers to make sure he was free when she came to the front of the line, dragging out a conversation or pushing coins and stamps into their hands. After a month of thirty-second conversations he knew more about Karen than she had ever volunteered to a person outside a letter.

"For your parents?" Ted asked, noticing the Newfoundland address on the envelope.

Karen shook her head no. "For my mother."

"Your father is dead?"

She smiled at him. "No, no, just not much of a letter person."

Ted's face was cherubic and uncomplicated, like the face of a child before it learns to disguise emotion. "You are very lucky," he advised her. "Since I have come to Canada, my parents are no longer living." He smiled up at her quickly, to be clear he wasn't looking for sympathy.

"How did you end up here?" Karen asked him, waving her hand to indicate the building, the city, the country.

"My parents worked very hard to send me to school. I have been living with my uncle here for several years. He is a 'big man' with the corporation," he said, waving his hand to indicate the building. "I work part time here to help pay my way through university."

Karen licked her stamps and stuck them on the envelope, hammering them into place with the heel of her palm. "That's a better story than mine," she admitted. "I just stuck a pin in a map."

"Not true!" Ted shouted.

"True," Karen insisted, nodding her head. She leaned across the counter towards him. "Actually, the first place I hit was somewhere in northern Saskatchewan, but I didn't think I could stomach it. I love being so close to the lake here."

On one particularly slow morning at the post office, Karen learned that Ted's name was not Ted but Hong Gu Li. On the day he arrived in Canada the airport customs official, after asking his name several times, finally threw up his hands in frustration. "I understand you're *hun-ger-y* young man, but we have to get through this paperwork before you can eat." His uncle convinced him a Chinese name would be an impediment in his adopted country and immediately christened him "Ted."

"That's ridiculous," Karen interrupted. "Why *Ted*, for God's sake?"

Ted shrugged. "It was the first name that came to his mind. And now Ted is what I am to live with. I never told my mother and father. I am afraid they would have been disappointed in me."

Every time Karen and Ted met, he talked about his parents in a solemn and reverent manner that made Karen jealous. "Did they love each other?" she asked him.

"Of course," he said, surprised by the question. "My parents were married in China, years before they left for Taiwan. They were promised to one another by my grandparents when they were children."

There was something about the notion of an arranged marriage that appealed to Karen, although it lurked so far beneath the repulsion she felt that she didn't recognize or acknowledge it. "I think we have very different ideas of love," she said.

Ted nodded his head and smiled at her. "You are a woman," he said. "I am a man." He held his hands above the counter for a moment and shrugged.

Karen thought she couldn't possibly find someone more completely her opposite, someone more unselfconscious and trusting, someone so blindly optimistic.

It became obvious to Karen over time that her parents were deeply in love and would have been miserably unhappy without one another. She thinks it was this realization more than anything else that put her off the idea of romance as a young girl.

Her father kept up a barrage of insults and taunts out of mere habit, never expecting any response from his wife beyond her customary sarcasm. He'd surrendered any hope of provoking anger or retaliation years ago, but still flew the flag of ridicule in the stiff breeze of her mother's good-natured dismissiveness. He marched through the living room waving a handful of bills like evidence in a court case, his wiry arms miming fury. "Your mother," he would explain to Karen for the ten-thousandth time, "is the kind of woman who buys herself a handbag, and then decides she needs a dress to match the frigging handbag."

It was never clear to Karen how much truth there was to her father's accusations. Her mother didn't even bother to argue the point. "Just crack open another one of those money barrels in the basement my love, and stop being such a cheap arsehole."

"You hear that," he said, still talking to his daughter. "Now what am I supposed to do with an attitude like that?"

Her mother pursed her lips and blew him a kiss across the room.

"Don't go trying to suck up to me," he warned her, waving the handful of bills in her direction, a smile just beginning to crest the look of reproach on his face.

Karen supposes a lesser person than her mother would have been driven to distraction, if not outright despair. It helped that she was a large woman, it added to her sense of indestructibility. Karen was twiggy and slight, her slenderness giving her an air of fragility she couldn't disguise. Her father, in his way, found fault with them both. She was emaciated, a weakling. He was always after her to eat more, to put a little meat on her bones. "Sweet sacred heart of Jesus," he muttered, "nothing that tiny could have come out of your mother, there must have been a mix up at the hospital." Her mother on the other hand was constantly urged to diet. "We'll have to bury you in a fucking piano case if you keep this up," he told her as he watched her eat. Her mother would smile around her mouthful of salt beef or spaghetti while she chewed and swallowed slowly. "My darling," she said, "the more I eat, the more of me there is to love."

Karen and Ted met every Sunday lunch for dim sum at a local Chinese restaurant, Ted teaching her how to use chopsticks, explaining the Chinese zodiac. He ate nothing but *jiaotzi*, tiny dumplings stuffed with pork and vegetable, popping them into his mouth whole and speaking as he chewed. "I was born," he began without preamble, "in the Year of the Dragon. I am excitable and temperamental. I am honest and extremely loyal. And you were born?"

"In 1965."

"Oh ho," Ted shouted, his chopsticks held aloft like a conductor's baton at the start of a symphony. "The Year of the Snake. We call the snake the Little Dragon," he went on. Then, in a whisper, leaning across the table toward her, "Of course, we are a very bad match. We will fight constantly." He smiled, and Karen thought for a moment she should explain about her parents. She had no idea where to begin.

"And who," she asked instead, "will win these fights?"

"Why Little Dragon," he said, his eyes wide to imply the answer was obvious. "Of course it will be me."

Ted's first "victory" came with the question of whether or

not they should go "all the way." "I am an old-fashioned man," he told her, "a patient man. I will wait."

They were lying together in her bed, completely naked but for their socks. "Come on!" Karen said, "You call this old fashioned?" But Ted would not be moved. She pressed her face into his chest, cupping her hand around his nearly hairless testicles, the weight of them resting in her palm. "If my father was as patient a man as yourself," she told him, "I probably wouldn't be here at all."

When Karen's parents married, her mother was only nineteen and already three months pregnant. Karen discovered this when she was thirteen by counting the months backwards from her birthday to the wedding date, and she spent a lot of time afterwards creating elaborate and completely speculative stories to explain this. Her father forced himself upon her mother and she was driven to marriage by her pregnancy. She had too much to drink on her nineteenth birthday and slept with her father in a stupor. She felt sorry for her father (a not overly handsome, not overly intelligent man) and slept with him out of pity. She was impregnated by her true love, Mr. Varley, who broke up with her before it became apparent, forcing her to marry the first eligible bachelor she could find, a slightly older man with bad teeth, little money, and no prospects.

In each scenario, Karen's mother was the nearly-innocent girl forced into a marriage of convenience by desperate circumstance. Her father was either a villain or a piece of furniture, a man caught up in events he neither controlled nor comprehended. It seemed impossible for

Karen to think of him in any other way. She couldn't fathom what her mother saw in her father or why she had let Mr. Varley slip away. To her mind, the post master seemed altogether more credible as a possible husband and father, less cartoonish and offensive. "Mom," she said one evening. "Why didn't you and Mr. Varley get married?"

Her mother settled onto the bed where Karen was sitting, the sway of the mattress tipping her daughter into the crook of her arm. "Now princess," her mother said into her hair, "who told you Mr. Varley and I were ever thinking of getting married?"

Karen shrugged uncomfortably. "It was in your high school yearbook."

"Is that a fact. And where did you find my high school yearbook?"

"In a box in the basement."

"Mmm," her mother said, nodding her head.

Karen looked up at her. Her features were blunted slightly by her heaviness, which made it difficult to read her expression. A dark mole sat at the base of her throat like an elegant brooch. "So why didn't you?" Karen asked.

"Well," she said without pausing, "I met your father."

"Mom," Karen whined. "You broke up with Mr. Varley for *Dad*?"

"That's my story," her mother said, heaving herself up from the bed. "And I'm sticking to it." She kissed the top of her daughter's head. "And you, my darling girl, are the happy ending to it all."

Before she fell asleep that night, Karen concocted this scenario: Mr. Varley breaking up with her mother (Was he mad about something? Was there another woman?), her mother sleeping with her father to make Mr. Varley jealous (ok, that was a stretch), followed immediately by the pregnancy and the speedy marriage and voila.

It was a comfort to think of herself as an accident. It freed her from the inevitability of being exactly who she was.

Karen was nine years old the first time she left home. Her mother was at the Legion playing Bingo. Her father was in the living room staring at the Saturday night hockey game.

Karen had been watching a documentary on the Labrador Innu when he walked into the room and flipped the channel. She was lying on the carpet and he stepped over her to sit in the easy chair. She stood between him and the television, staring.

"What?" he asked her. His face had the smugly startled look of an actor rehearsing an encounter with a harmless ghost.

"I was watching that," she said, her fists on her tiny hips.

"Watching what?"

"The Eskimos."

"Well look," he said, pointing at the television behind her. "This is just the same, a bunch of savages on ice. Look out now, for jesussake, so I can see."

She really did hate him, hated his willful stupidity, hated his carelessness. Tiger Williams was digging for a puck in the corner when she pulled on her coat and boots and slipped quietly through the front door. She began walking out of Black Rock, past the yellow glow in the windows of the houses at the edge of the townsite. She stepped through the silver pool of light thrown by the town's last street lamp, not knowing where she was going, too furious to care. The nearest town was thirty miles north. The stars glittered against the night sky like pins on a map of black felt. She wanted to keep walking until she was in another life. Her tears were freezing on her cheeks, her feet and mittened fingers numb with the cold. If she walked long enough she thought her entire body might die around her, slough off like an old skin.

She had passed the turn off to Beothuk Lake when the headlights of the pickup found her on the roadside. Her father leaned across to open the passenger door and Karen stepped up into the seat. Neither of them spoke. She leaned her head against the window as he turned and drove back towards the lights of Black Rock, her hands and feet prickling with pain as feeling slowly returned to them.

When Karen decided to end her relationship with Ted she made the announcement at their weekly dim sum lunch. And although she thought she had prepared sufficiently, rehearsing a speech like a lawyer before a jury summation, she couldn't properly explain what she was afraid of. The more time they spent together the more it seemed their relationship was preordained, that her life was destined to be this thing and not another. "It's just impossible," she said with a defiant, defeated shrug in her voice, as if she had spent months trying to master Rubic's Cube and was finally dismissing it as a pointless exercise.

Ted didn't say a word through her entire presentation, sitting with his arms folded stoically, his eyes focused on the empty white plate before him. When he was sure she had finished he reached for the bowl of *jiaotzi*. "I am a patient man," he told her as he chewed. "I believe there is such a thing as fate. My parents survived terrible times before they escaped to Taiwan. Now I am here and I have met you. These things are not accidents. I will wait."

His confidence infuriated her. "You *will* wait," she told him. "You'll wait a long, long time."

When the time came, it wasn't a piano case but an urn the size of a flower pot that carried her mother to her final resting place.

Coming as it did, less than a month after Karen broke up with Ted, her mother's death was like a flame striking gasoline. Her whole world, such as it was, had come apart. She was too numb even to resent her father's nastiness. "No surprise," he told her on the drive home from the airport in Gander. "I told her she was going to kill herself eating like that. Like jumping up and down on a goddamn landmine."

Karen leaned her head against the window of the pickup, barely listening. The alder and birch along the roadside were stripped naked, their grey trunks and limbs looked emaciated and helpless against the sky.

There were no crematoria facilities in Black Rock so the body was shipped to Grand Falls for the ceremony and burning. Her mother insisted on cremation, her father said, because she wanted to avoid the embarrassment of doing permanent injury to the pallbearers. According to the will, the ashes were to be scattered over the water of Beothuk Lake, just outside of town. Her father pulled at the oars while Karen sat facing him, the urn held firmly between her knees. She avoided his eyes, looking past his shoulder at the opposite shore.

"Far enough, I s'pose," he said finally. "I don't know why she got on with all this foolishness, she never liked the water much anyways."

It made Karen feel empty to hear him talk, it was like listening to one half of a conversation. "Here alright?" she asked, leaning out over the gunnel.

"Bombs away," he said, flinging one arm in that direction.

She shook the ashes into the water, a fine film of dust blowing back onto the sleeve of her coat. She set the urn down and brushed the sleeve off over the water, then watched the grey spores drift away, half of what had made her scattered now and gone. It made her think of Ted suddenly, of the first time he had ejaculated into her hand, the white net of cum warm against her skin, those millions of possibilities spilled on her fingertips. She felt overwhelmed by the thought of how many things a person ends up saying no to in life.

Her father turned the boat and began pulling for shore. The wind was light but cold, his fingers red as autumn leaves on the oars. "Never thought I'd see the day your mother would float," he said. Karen turned her head to say something, but stopped short when she saw the film of tears and the unexpected grey look of grief on his face. She looked back to the water, biting the inside of her lip until she tasted blood, and stared at the spot where her mother was raining slowly toward the bottom of the lake.

When they reached shallow water her father stepped from the boat and pulled the keel up onto the beach, dragging it out of the lake completely after Karen got out beside him. She helped him turn it face down on the sand and they stood watching the calm surface of the water. Her father took out his handkerchief and blew his nose, wiped quickly at his red-rimmed eyes and then pushed the cloth into his back pocket.

"This is where we used to come," he said. "When we were youngsters you know, not even your age hardly. We'd have a fire going and a few beers down here, a blanket on the sand." He stopped suddenly as if he had forgotten the rest of the story and stared at his feet, an awkward grin on his face, a flush spreading across his cheeks. "I never knew what your mother saw in me, first or last. I was just lucky I guess."

Karen looked at him carefully, at his ball cap and bent shoulders, his ears the size of pears, at the lean body that was hers as well. "I was an accident," she said, feeling absolutely certain of that fact now, but no longer sure it signified anything important. "Wasn't I, Dad?" she said.

Her father shook his head slowly, still staring out over the water. "My darling girl," he said. He held the arm of her jacket for a moment, then let his hand drop back to his side.

She touched her tongue to the tiny wound inside her mouth. In a city she had chosen by sticking a pin in a map there was a man from another country waiting for her. She had no idea if that was fate or blind luck, and she supposed that in the end it made little difference either way. It was what she had.

BREAK & ENTER

Shari used to think of it as her sister's story, as "what happened to Aria." As if a story could be about one thing and one thing only. Aria says no, it's her story too, that even when she was absent Shari was involved. Her face there, then not there, like a moon moving through clouds.

Aria was throwing things. Anything she could get her hands on, shoes, books, a fork. She was chasing Alan through the house, throwing the lid of a paint can, a paint brush, the telephone that reached part way across the living room and came up short like a running dog on a chain. She was screaming at him, *bastard, you prick, you lousy fucker.* She chased him through one room after another as he held his hands helplessly in front of his face, trying to explain or apologize. She couldn't stand the sight of the man, his tired eyes, his look of complete defeat. She threw a coffee cup, an apple from a bowl of fruit. She hated him and couldn't imagine ever feeling any other way about him. She picked up the phone and threw it in the other direction and it clanged stupidly against the wall.

"Jesus, Aria!" Alan said.

When she was too tired to throw anything else she sat on the floor and cried helplessly. "I want you out," she said. "Now," she told him. "I want you out."

"Please, Aria," Alan begged. He was sitting in the hallway

just out of her sight, and he was crying too now. "Please," he said. "I'm so scared. Please help me."

This was in the spring of their first year in the new house. Shari had never met Alan, and didn't know yet that her sister was living with someone, or any of the things that had happened between them.

There's a certain character of light, Aria says, an afternoon light through windows holding particles of dust, that brings the whole thing back to her. The kind of light she remembers from weekends in August, when they'd just moved in—the garden out back overgrown, trees moving in the breeze, the rooms of the house luminous with sunshine. She felt overcome by it sometimes, every inch of her skin seemed to glow beneath her clothes, as if her body was lit from the inside.

It's nostalgia Shari hears in her sister's voice more and more now, regret. As if she's almost run out of horror stories to tell and has unexpectedly rediscovered these sweet moments, like coins found under the cushions of a sofa during a cleaning binge.

She liked to spend Saturday afternoons in the garden, weeding, watering, her hands wrist deep in the warm soil. Alan was in the house, working in his white undershirt with dabs of paint drying on his forearms, the dust of sanded wood in his hair. The thought of him inside was like a voice calling and calling until she couldn't resist it any longer, walking into the house then, already tasting him: the sheen of sweat on his neck, the sweet taste of apples from his mouth he could never explain to her. They made love wherever she found him, on the drop sheets spread across the floor in the spare room, on the chesterfield, in the kitchen. Aria came almost as soon as he was inside her or his tongue slipped between the swollen lips of her labia.

When Aria was a girl, her mother had always talked to her plants. "It isn't enough just to water them once a week," she explained to her daughters. "You have to let them know you care." Shari simply rolled her eyes, but Aria tried it a few times when she was alone in the house. "Hello," she said, as if introducing herself to a stranger. "My name is Aria. How do you do?" She'd felt ridiculous then, and it was the same somehow with Alan. He never questioned those afternoons, accepting what seemed almost a private ritual without comment. Aria wished he was more curious about it, wished he would pry at her the way he took the lid off a paint can. As soon as she opened her mouth to explain herself she felt awkward and unbalanced, as clumsy as a child in high heels. It was simpler just to lie there, tracing a finger along the firm ridge of the hockey scar on his chin, enjoying the heat of the sunlight touching their bodies.

Shari is most uncomfortable listening to these confessions, to the explicit descriptions of their love making, the admission of something embarrassingly close to bliss. For the rest of the afternoon, Aria says, she could feel the sweet buzz of their sex in her head, the warmth in her belly and between her legs as she continued working in the garden. There was a time, Aria says, and it makes Shari cringe to hear it, when she thought they would go on forever that way.

———

It was Shari's idea to paint the bathroom.

"Nothing feels worth it anymore," Aria told her on the phone, the cord choked around her index finger, the tip almost purple. "I don't see the point."

Shari was living in Montreal, only three hours from her sister. They hadn't seen each other since their mother's funeral more than two years before.

"Don't talk like that," Shari said. "Don't talk stupid. You'll get past this."

"Everywhere I look I see him. He renovated every fucking room, Shar. I can't avoid him in here."

The downstairs bathroom was the only room that Alan hadn't touched before he left, putting it off repeatedly because they hadn't been able to agree on a colour. He wanted something outrageous, aubergine he kept suggesting. She preferred something more traditional, white with blue trim, or a nice daffodil yellow. A marbled aqua was as adventurous as she was willing to get.

"Listen to me," Shari said. She was wondering if her sister's hair still reached the small of her back, if she still wore hoop earrings large enough to slip over your wrist. She felt as if she was trying to find a way into an abandoned house, prying at boarded windows. "Listen," she said again. "This is what I want you to do."

As soon as she hung up the phone, Aria walked to a downtown hardware store and ordered a gallon of eggshell white and a pint of soft blue. By the time she got home her arms were shaking from the weight of the paint cans, a knot of tension throbbing across her back. She changed into a pair of ripped jeans and an old t-shirt, tied her hair back with a kerchief. She found the drop sheets folded neatly in the basement, the brushes and rollers cleaned and placed on shelves beside the roll pans and a container of turpentine. She carried what she needed up to the bathroom and set everything on the floor. She looked at the mirrored medicine cabinet over the sink, saw herself staring back. "Alan always hated that thing," she said aloud, and she began cleaning the cabinet out, placing pill bottles and pink plastic razors and cough syrup on the floor. She picked the metal frame up off the wall screws and lifted it out over the sink, her tired arms shaking with the weight. The cabinet slipped from her hands then, hitting the porcelain sink and falling to the floor where the mirror shattered. Aria stood back from the mess, her hand clamped to her mouth. Among the shards was the needle that had been hidden over the medicine cabinet, the tip encrusted with blood.

When Aria first met him, Alan had been clean for six and a half years. He'd moved to the mainland to start over and set himself up as a handyman in Kingston, doing carpentry and plumbing along with a bit of interior design. He was recommended to Aria by a lawyer at the firm he'd done some drywalling for the previous summer. She had just purchased a small house in the city's north end with the little money her mother left in her will. It was a rental property that had been trashed by a succession of university students. Aria was planning to do some quick renovations so she could sell and put a downpayment on something larger downtown.

They walked through the living room and dining room together, Alan making calculations in his head. He pointed at the dark panelling. "Now, it's your money," he said, "but if it was me, I'd want to drywall all of this." He spoke rapidly, his words rear-ending one another like reckless cars on a busy street; his "th" was nearly emptied of sibilance, a flat "d" or "t." "Dese," he said, "tings." His accent made Aria feel immediately affectionate towards him.

Alan took a crowbar and ripped up an edge of the wood pannelling, tearing the whole sheet off with his hands. "That's all plaster and lathe underneath there," he told her, turning the crowbar around and banging at the wall. Chunks of plaster fell to the brown carpet and Aria winced slightly. "There's nothing you can do to a building that can't be fixed," he reassured her.

The renovations took eight weeks, Alan doing the work alone when he could. Aria came to the house from the lawyer's office every evening, bagging garbage, sanding the plaster over the drywall tape, amazed at the transformation. She watched Alan work, pulling out the pressboard cupboards in the kitchen, lifting a sheet of drywall to the ceiling on his shoulder, installing a new stainless steel sink.

"It's looking great," she told him, and he nodded vaguely in her direction. He was resolutely polite and professional whenever she was around, which drove her crazy. She practiced calling to invite him to a movie or a meal, talking aloud on her way to the office or in the shower, and the week before the renovations were completed she finally worked up the nerve to ask him out. He was four rungs up on a ladder when she suggested they go somewhere for a drink. He was wearing the white undershirt he stripped down to when the work got hot, and jeans, and unlaced workboots. He stopped what he was doing and climbed down from the ladder. Aria had been expecting a straight yes or no, and she found it difficult to stand still as she waited for Alan to find a chair and sit down. "How about it?" she said.

"I don't drink," Alan said finally. "Anymore."

"We could go for a sundae," Aria suggested, without much enthusiasm, already sorry she'd brought it up.

"I'm beat," Alan said. "Maybe some other time."

"OK, sure," she told him, turning away to find something to do with her hands. "Some other time. Sure."

She assumed that was the end of it. Three weeks later he showed up at her office just before lunch carrying two ice cream sundaes. "You like nuts?" he asked. "I got one with and one without."

They walked to a nearby park and Alan started in about Black Rock, about the drinking and then the drugs. He'd been a star hockey player in his home town, played on the provincial Midget and Junior teams. He was introduced to cocaine at a house party in Calgary at the end of the Air Canada Cup tournament, when he was fourteen. By the time the NHL scouts began visiting his parents he was already hooked on heroin, shooting up in the soles of his feet to hide the track marks from his coaches. At eighteen he attended the Red Wings spring training camp, and was unceremoniously shipped back to St. John's after ten disastrous days. He stayed there for the better part of two years, sleeping in alleyways and the stairwells of parking garages. He'd almost killed himself, he said. He told her about breaking and entering, about opening accounts and making toilet paper deposits at bank machines. "Blah, blah, blah," he said, as if he thought he was boring her. "Same old story. I haven't been with anyone since then, not really," he admitted. "I didn't trust myself, you know? I was afraid of what I'd do."

Aria looked at him sideways. She felt embarrassed and awkward, as if she had been offered an extravagant gift and had nothing to give in return. The attraction she'd felt for him at first was an uncomplicated thing, something she'd almost gotten over in the past three weeks. But in the space of those thirty minutes everything changed. Alan seemed as alone in the world as she was and it made him beautiful in her eyes, the way a scar sometimes distinguishes rather than disfigures a face. He'd touched something broken in her, and she felt she might fall in love with him, as if that would be an appropriate way to repay him. "My mother," she said. "My mother died a few months ago." But she felt ridiculous and didn't say anything more.

Aria stepped across the shards of broken mirror, the used needle, and sat in the living room. She turned on the television she had retrieved from the pawn shop for seventy-five dollars. She flipped through channels without seeing what was on the screen. The needle shouldn't have been a surprise. He'd kept them hidden all over the house, above cupboards, in the toilet flush box, in the basement.

The television had been the last straw. He'd found her in the garden that afternoon, her knees brown with dirt, a dark rainbow of soil under her nails. She couldn't decide if she was surprised to see him or not. It had been weeks since they had spoken. She looked at him without getting up, without speaking a word. His hair had greyed, his face was aged and skeletal. His eyes were sunken and bruised by fatigue, and they looked to her like a pair of dark, expiring stars.

"I've had enough Aria," he said.

She stood up, slipping her bare feet into her Birkenstocks and she walked past him into the house, leaving the door open behind her.

"Where have you been?" she asked him.

"Please," he said without looking at her, "not now."

"Have you been sleeping on the street?"

"Not now."

"I'll make you something to eat."

"I just need to rest for a bit. Alright? Give me a shout in an hour. We'll talk." He went upstairs to the loft bedroom and Aria stood in the kitchen for a few minutes, bewildered. Light streamed through the windows, dust hanging in the air. She looked at the dirt under her fingernails and then walked back out to the garden. She tried not to think of him lying in the upstairs bed, concentrated on the task at hand, turning forkfuls of soil, squishing white cabbage slugs between her fingers.

An hour later she went back into the house to wake him. She called his name as she walked into the living room, stopping suddenly when she saw the door onto the street standing open. She heard the hiss of traffic outside, the voices of children on bicycles, all of the sounds muffled as if she were hearing them from under water. She looked around the room and knew before she saw it, that the television had been taken from its stand in the corner.

After she retrieved the set from the pawn shop, she emptied his clothes out of the drawers in the bedroom and took them to the Salvation Army. She called her sister and told her everything: the house, Alan's history, the money missing from her coat pockets, the credit cards from her purse, the bank account being emptied, creditors calling about outstanding bills for building materials.

"Jesus," Shari whispered. "How long has this been going on?"

"I don't know. Since last spring. Over a year."

"Have you laid charges?"

"I feel like I'm moving in slow motion, Shar. Like I'm under water. I haven't even called the police yet."

"Jesus, Aria, you work for a lawyer. You should know better."

The anger in Shari's voice was so sudden and intense that it was almost soothing, like the sound of rain on a rooftop, and Aria began crying into the receiver. "You don't understand," she said. "You don't know him."

"He's damaged goods, Aria. Please, honey. Call the police." Shari was on her feet and pacing the floor. She stretched the phone cord as close to the door as it would reach and pulled on her shoes as she spoke. "I'm driving down," she said. "Have you changed the locks yet?"

After that first conversation, Shari made a point of calling Aria once or twice a week. Early one Saturday morning a man answered the phone. Shari was so surprised she almost hung up. "Who is this?" she asked.

The man laughed dismissively. "Who's *this?*"

"I'm looking for Aria. I'm her sister."

"Oh, Shari, right? I've heard a lot about you."

Shari stood up from her chair. "Is this Alan? What are you doing there?"

"Aria's in the yard," Alan said cheerfully. "Hang on a sec." She heard the door open, and the muffled sound of him shouting. "Ok," he was saying. "Uh huh." He lifted the phone back to his mouth. "She's face and eyes into the garden, Shar. You know what she's like. Can she call you back in half an hour?"

"Um," Shari said. "Sure, I guess." What the hell was Aria thinking, she wondered.

"Bye now," Alan said, and he hung up.

She stood with the sound of the dial tone in her ear for a moment before it hit her. "Fuck," she muttered. "Fuck, fuck, fuck." She redialed Aria's number. No answer. She hung up, redialed, stabbing the keypad with her index finger. The lying bastard. The prick, the lousy fucker. The answering service clicked in, Aria's recorded voice talking calmly in her ear. Shari slammed the phone on the floor.

She grabbed her keys and took the stairs of her apartment building two at a time. She hit stop and go traffic on her way out of the downtown core and she realized how useless it was to rush to her sister's place. Anything that might be happening at this moment would be long over by the time she arrived, but there was nothing else she could think to do. She stopped at every service station along the 401 and left the same message on Aria's machine. "I'm coming," she said. "I'll be there as soon as I can."

Aria was sitting in the middle of the living room floor when Shari walked into the house. She had a bucket of neapolitan ice cream between her legs. "Comfort food," she explained.

"You ok?"

Aria shrugged. "I went out to the corner store. He must have been waiting in the garden. Broke in through the back window," she said, pointing with her spoon.

Shari sat across from her sister. Aria had put her hair into two Pippi Longstocking braids that hung on either side of her face, the way her mother liked her to wear it when she was a girl. She offered a spoonful of ice cream and Shari leaned toward her for a taste. The cold made her teeth ache.

Aria rooted in the ice cream container. "Thanks for coming," she said.

Shari looked away from her, lifting her head to scan around the room. "Did he touch you?"

"I missed him altogether." Her tone was light, exhilarated, as if she had miraculously survived a plane crash. "He got the laptop and the VCR. That was all he could carry I imagine." She offered the spoon again. "More?"

Shari shook her head. "Why did he answer the phone?"

Aria shrugged. "He was probably pretty strung out. Reflex maybe."

Shari shook her head and laughed in disbelief. "You're kidding!"

Aria laughed along with her, trying to hold in a mouthful of ice cream. "Nope," she managed.

Shari felt it too then, how ludicrous the whole affair was, how none of it made sense. Another time something like this would make her feel like crying, but at the moment the only logical thing to do was laugh. She and Aria went into hysterics, feeding off one another. Shari slapped the hardwood floor with her palm until it ached.

On the first Saturday in the new house, Aria had come in from the garden and found Alan on his knees in the living room, tearing out the old baseboard. She knelt behind him, pulling up his shirt, kissing the bare skin, brushing her nipples across his back. He turned toward her with a startled expression and she kissed him then, slipping her tongue into his mouth before he could say anything.

"I'm thinking of a dark umber for the back wall," he said afterwards, lying in her arms on the floor.

Aria looked around the room as if she was considering, her index finger twirling the tuft of dark hair below his navel. "What colour is umber exactly?" she asked.

"Nevermind," he said. "I'll pick up some swatches next week."

"Swatches?"

"Nevermind," he said again, laughing.

There was a pause between them, as if they had both turned over in their minds and lay with their backs to one another.

"Alan," she said, "where did the drugs come from?" She tugged at his pubic hair nervously, as if she was trying to extract a confession. "I mean, I don't understand what got you into it."

"What's to understand?" Alan said, shifting uncomfortably. "You know as much as I do already. Family stuff, personal stuff. Stupidity. There's nothing more to say really." He sat up slowly, reaching for his shirt. He could tell from the look on her face that she wasn't satisfied. "Listen," he said, "another person in my place would have done things differently. Maybe," he said flippantly, "it's my calling."

The fact that there was no single traumatic event at the root of the problem frightened her. It meant that Alan was more than the sum of what she knew of him. For a moment she watched him clawing at the baseboard with a crowbar as if he was a total stranger. "Hello," she felt like saying, "my name is Aria. How do you do?" She placed her hand on the inside of her thigh, moving her fingers through the small resinous pool of Alan's cum on her skin, the liquid already cool to the touch. She brought her fingertips to her mouth, dabbing them against her tongue, surprised to find they were almost completely tasteless.

The first and last time Shari laid eyes on Alan was a warm Saturday in June. She was visiting from Montreal. She and Aria went downtown early, eating brunch at a small cafe and then browsing through fabric stores and flower shops. Aria hadn't spoken to Alan in months, she had no idea if he was in the city, or if he was even alive. They stopped at the window of a furniture store and Shari watched her sister there beside her, the straight brown hair under a straw hat, the gold hoop earrings almost touching her shoulders.

They were about to turn away when Aria saw him, when she saw the reflection of him, passing on the opposite side of the street: the lanky gait, the white undershirt and jeans. Her first thought was, "He has a beard now," and then she couldn't seem to think at all.

Shari called her sister's name, but Aria had already turned in Alan's direction, following his head bobbing in a crowd of afternoon shoppers, running to try and stay abreast of him, waiting for a chance to cross the street between traffic. Her hat blew off her head and she stopped to pick it up, clutching it in her hand as she ran.

Shari was following behind her, shouting at her sister to stop. Aria crossed the street, and then turned a corner out of sight. Shari stepped onto the pavement, waiting for a chance to follow. She swore under her breath at the steady line of traffic. She shouted her sister's name again.

When she found her, Aria was sitting on the sidewalk crying, her hat and handbag between her knees. Alan was nowhere in sight. Shari stood beside her and looked up and down the street. "Jesus, Aria," she whispered.

Later that afternoon, Aria went to the basement and carried up rags, rollers, paint thinner, the half a can of egg shell white left over from the bathroom. She set everything on the living room floor and stared at the dark umber wall.

Shari was sitting on the grass in the shade of the fence. She could see Aria working through the living room window, her hair tied back, dabs of paint scarring her shoulders and face. Almost two hours passed before Aria came outside and sat beside her. Her back was sore, her fingers stinging from the paint thinner she used to wipe them clean. She reached across to hold Shari's hand and closed her eyes, picturing the back wall of the living room freshly painted. She could smell the grass underneath her, and perfumed soap on her sister's skin, and the sharp scent of turpentine on her hands and in the air around them.

PRAXIS

Sometimes Clara thinks a family is just an excuse for cruelty. Usually she thinks this after she and Jacob have fought about something, if she's had to take him to bed by the ear, or he won't finish his supper and she refuses to let him watch *Teenage Mutant Ninja Turtles* in retaliation. But that feeling, the one in the pit of her stomach when she's afraid she's acting like her mother or father, doesn't last long. Sometimes she thinks it isn't fair to herself, sometimes she thinks it isn't fair to her parents. "Lay down," she says, like she's talking to a skittish animal familiar with her voice. More often than not, it does.

Clara was twenty-two when her mother left for good, moving back to St. Lawrence where she found a job tending bar at the Legion Hall. It didn't pay much, but she was saving her tips toward a trip somewhere, maybe Florida, maybe the Grand Canyon, she hadn't decided yet. Clara was working at the Company staff office in Black Rock and had a place of her own by this point. Eric was teaching English as a Second Language somewhere in South America, Columbia or Ecuador, she couldn't remember which.

Clara and Jacob moved back in with her father after he had spent a couple of months on his own. If anyone asked, she said she was trying to save money, but the truth was she didn't think her father was capable of taking care of himself. He seemed to deflate slightly after the break-up, his customary bluster and coldness shifted to something more like bewilderment. He went on working at the mine, spending his free time drinking at the Union Hall or lost in the television. But there were days when he sat staring blankly for hours, as if he were going over his whole life, piece by piece, trying to fit it together in a way that might make sense of things.

When Clara does this, when she tries to make a story of it with a beginning, a middle and an end, she comes back to one October afternoon during the '72 strike as the point where she felt it coming apart for good. She'd just come home from school, her father was on shift at the picket line. Her mother was usually cooking supper by this time, or watching "As The World Turns" in the living room with a cigarette and a gingerale, but there was no sign of her. Clara called to her as she pulled off her shoes in the porch. She walked into the kitchen over the cool linoleum in her white stocking feet, her hand reaching automatically for the door of the refrigerator, calling again.

She remembers the shock of the unexpected resistance, the weird metallic rattle. There was a length of chain looped through the door-handle; a cheap padlock from the Imperial General Store held it around the thick waist of the refrigerator, the soft lips of the door clamped shut.

The walk-out at the mine was well into its fifth month. Negotiations broke down after the first two weeks, with each side blaming the other for leaving the table. The strikers and their families were surviving on sixty dollars a month, plus two dollars a week per child. The Premier of Newfoundland, facing increasing unpopularity and a looming election, became the first government official to publicly criticize the Company's labour practices since the mine was established in the 1920s. In the Toronto *Globe and Mail*, he referred to ASAMCo as a "nineteenth-century company" and "a poor corporate citizen," hoping to goad management back to the table and score points with voters, without success on either count.

The strikers set up stone barricades at the dam and picketed the main entrance twenty-four hours a day. Over a period of weeks, all the windows in the Company's office buildings were broken out. After a train caboose was burnt to the wheels by strikers, two dozen RCMP officers were dispatched from St. John's to assist the single policeman stationed in town.

The Company printed up a flyer and sent it around to every house in town. The union-management relationship, it said, was akin to a marriage—complicated but mutually beneficial—and it was in the best interests of both parties if problems were discussed rationally and openly. They appealed to people's sense of decency, requesting that level-heads prevail during these difficult times.

No one had ever heard of such a thing. The union grieved the flyer as a breach of the collective bargaining process. Clara's father found it amusing and infuriating at the same time. He sat at the kitchen table in his white undershirt, his free hand circling the bald pate of his head as he read and re-read the flyer. "They're right about the marriage thing, the bastards," he said finally. "They've been screwing us for years and now they're in for one hell of a spat."

Clara assumes that's where her mother got the idea, but she's only guessing.

Her mother's best friend, Charlene Pottle, answered the phone when Clara called. "Betty," Charlene said over her shoulder, "it's Clara."

"You tell your father," her mother said, "that I don't cook another meal, and I don't spend another night in that house until he books a ticket to Florida. You just tell him that."

It wasn't travel her mother wanted, Clara thinks, so much as escape. Florida was just a word, the name of some place she'd never been. She'd always spoken of it in a wistful "what if" way as she washed dishes or put away a bag full of groceries. Clara's father didn't even acknowledge the request, absently scratching at his forearm or leaning toward the television screen to hear the weather forecast. Something ignored long enough, he believed, would go away eventually.

Their summer vacations didn't vary from one year to the next. They visited her father's mother near Harbour Grace, and her mother's parents in St Lawrence. Then they crossed the island to spend a week camping in the Codroy Valley. Hours cooped up in the car, her mother and father in the front seat like diplomats from countries involved in an ongoing dispute. Clara began conversations about anything neutral, the condition of the road, towns they passed through. She initiated travel games: who could be the first to guess the colour of approaching cars, the next out-of-province license plate? Even these eventually dissolved into arguments, or sly and petty insults about eyesight.

Eric, as usual, was lost in a book, or was sleeping with his head against a window, his glasses perched precariously at the end of his nose. His blank face shook with the rough movement of the car, as if he was experiencing a mild epileptic seizure. Sometimes Clara felt like slapping his glasses off his face.

They reached the park just after dusk. Eric and her father set up the camper, while Clara helped her mother cook a meal by the hissing light of a gas lantern. "This isn't a vacation," she'd say to Clara, standing over a frying pan on the Coleman stove, waving away mosquitos with the metal spatula. As far as she was concerned, camping was much like the rest of her life, with fewer conveniences. "What I wouldn't give for a decent beach," she muttered.

The Valley was a series of low rolling fields that was clear of the broken stone and tangle of roots that covered almost the entire island. Summer storms off the Gulf of St. Lawrence were common, without so much as a shrub to offer shelter from the gale force winds that threatened to topple tents and campers. Every other year, it seemed, her father and Eric would have to climb out into a vicious thunder storm and lash ropes over the top of the camper to keep it upright. Clara would never admit it to her mother, but she was exhilarated by those nights: the pistol shot crack of canvas on the camper frame, the dark rumble of thunder. All four of them lay awake, not speaking, both separated and connected by the noise and the darkness.

She looked forward to the cool evenings spent outside beside a fire after supper was cleared away, the night closing over them like a tarp of black felt. Eric tormented his father into singing the old songs, joining in on the choruses of the ones he remembered, "The Star of Logy Bay" and "Lukey's Boat," bits and pieces of "The Kelligrew's Soiree." Even her mother, who grew up singing in the United Church choir, accompanied them on a few, adding a warbly harmony to her father's almost tuneless voice; the shadows and moving light of the flames on her face bringing a younger face to the surface. Sometimes they would be joined by people from neighbouring campsites, a stranger walking out of the darkness into the red glow of the fire carrying a guitar and a lawn chair or an open bottle of beer, drawn to the music like moths to a candle.

Clara knew it was her father's stubbornness that kept them returning to the Valley, but there were things about it she'd come to enjoy. Eventually, she learned to dismiss her mother's complaints in much the same way her father did.

And then there was the chain on the fridge, the streaks of grease it had dragged across the cool white surface. Clara stared at it as she waited for her father to come home from the picket line. She thought of her mother's anger and how strong it must have been, how often she must have pegged it down, roped herself tight to avoid being carried away by the force of it.

Clara's brother had always been more aloof from the family battles than she could manage, retreating to his room with a book, losing himself in the American Civil War or the French Revolution. Clara wasn't as shrewd or as self-absorbed and she became a kind of envoy between her parents, a child forced into an impossible adult role.

Her relationship with Eric, on the other hand, was predictably, almost relentlessly, ordinary, at least on the surface.

He was four years older and they had little to do with one another. Their interactions tended to be brief and amicable, as if they were tenants of neighbouring apartments. But there was also something clandestine and unspoken between the two, something covert.

At eleven and a half, Clara bloodied her bed sheets and woke up screaming for her mother. She'd heard rumours at school, vague comments in washrooms about pads and spotting, but she had no idea what they meant. She could tell it was something secret and unpleasant, something as illicit as sex, but definitely to be avoided if possible. Leona Quinlan said it had something to do with babies, but that was as much as she knew.

Her mother didn't say a word when she came into Clara's bedroom, just shook her head solemnly, her once delicate features creased by a bruised look of disapproval. She brought her daughter to the bathroom and put a box of belted pads in her hand. "Read the instructions," she said and went out, pulling the door shut behind her.

That afternoon, Eric placed a book under her pillow, something he'd found at the public library called *Almost Thirteen*. There were pencil drawings of boys and girls with and without pubic hair, chapters on dating and sex, discussions about wet dreams and menstruation. She imagined him sneaking it up to the desk among a stack of history books, one about Napoleon maybe and one about the Great Irish Potato Famine, Mrs. Tucker looking furtively up at him over the rim of her spectacles before she stamped the return date in the back.

In her last year of high school, the year she had her first steady boyfriend, Eric had given her a copy of *Jonathon Livingston Seagull* as a graduation present. There was an envelope marked "Open in Private!!" between the pages. Inside she found three condoms in their square tin-foil wrappers. She remembers the embarrassment of his conspiratorial consent, the shame of it. And she remembers thinking about what he didn't know, what no one knew yet but her.

It was Eric who got her through the worst of the pregnancy. And it was Eric who supported her when she refused to marry the father, something both her parents had insisted on.

In the face of their parents' ongoing hostilities and sulking retreats, Clara and her brother had discovered a bond, an unusual sense of solidarity. Much later, Eric said it had been his first experience with class analysis. "There's no substitute for praxis," he said. Honest to God, Clara thought, sometimes it's like he speaks a different language.

What brought her mother home was the strike.

When her father finished his shift on the picket line that afternoon, he sat at the kitchen table, buffing the shiny pate of his crown with his palm and shaking his head in amazement. Even to suggest a vacation in the middle of a strike was ludicrous, inconceivable. They could barely afford to feed themselves. He seemed almost pleased by his wife's outrageous behaviour, the desperation of it, the uselessness.

Eventually he resolved to wait her out, to carry on as if nothing out of the ordinary had happened. He decided to warm up a can of soup for their supper, but when he went to the cupboard he found it had been glued shut. Every cupboard in the kitchen was sealed, including the cutlery drawers.

"And a good goddamn thing too," he yelled, growing

more and more furious as he moved from one door to another, "because if I could get my hands on a knife right now I'd have her black heart for supper!" Clara tried to calm him down, but only succeeded in making things worse. "Don't you go taking her side in this!" he told her. He slammed out the door and headed for the Pottle's place. Clara sat on the floor in the kitchen, fighting an almost uncontrollable urge to cry. She thought of calling her brother in St. John's, but she had no idea what to tell him.

She was still sitting there when her father walked back in the door. Charlene's husband had intercepted him as he'd arrived: Betty didn't want to talk to her husband at the moment, Lester Pottle told him. He should go home and try to cool down, Lester said. Her father didn't speak or acknowledge Clara for the rest of the night. He sat alone in the cold blue light of the television, a furious silence hedging his body like the aureole of a star.

There was a lot of talk about it on the picket line after that. The union's strike fund was almost depleted and the first weeks of collective rage had settled into a more sullen and less-focused sense of frustration. There were shoving matches over cigarettes, vehement arguments pitting the skills of the current Montreal Canadiens against those of the 60s' Maple Leafs.

Her father and Lester had to be moved to separate shifts on the line and one by one the other men began taking sides. Most of them felt Lester had no right to interfere in a private dispute and should send Clara's mother home. Others thought he had no real say in the matter and was just making the best of a bad situation. The debate threatened to break down the little collective resolve the men had left.

Even the kids at school were talking about it. Leona Quinlan passed on the gossip during recess as they shared a cigarette behind the school. "Jackie Houtman says something must be going on between your mother and Mr. Pottle," Leona said. Clara took a long helpless drag, feeling the smoke curl to the bottom of her lungs and burrow in there. "And Rod Harris says no, there must be something going on between your mother and *Mrs.* Pottle." Leona shook her head. "I think I'd die if my parents were that weird," she said.

A week after her mother had locked the refrigerator shut, Clara came home from school to find her in the kitchen cooking supper. "There are some things," she said, "that are more important than Florida." And nothing more was said about it. When her father came home that evening, he sat down at the table without a word.

Clara thinks everyone knew it was only a temporary truce. That no one was surprised when it finally happened. Her parents didn't speak at all after the divorce went through. Clara kept in touch by telephone, but her mother didn't even ask after her father. He stood over Clara during the weekly calls just to make sure his life didn't become a topic of conversation.

Even after the tests confirmed the cancer, he refused to allow Clara to tell her mother what was happening. Sometimes she thought her father just didn't want to give her mother the satisfaction; other times she thought he wanted to be spared the pity. There was nothing to be done but wait, the doctors said. Too many years of cigarettes, too many shifts in the mine.

Clara was alone with him when he died. She stood at his side, brushing her hand against the hair on his forearm, its slight resistance against her fingers a small, physical comfort. He had been drugged into a state of near unconsciousness for the last hours of his life and even before he passed away Clara thought his face seemed strangely vacant against the blank hospital pillow, his body under the white sheets like a crate emptied of its contents. It made her think of a night in the Valley as she was making her way to bed in the camper, looking back at him from the doorway, at his silhouette between her and the fire. It was the first time she saw what it was her mother had been attracted to: a regular income, a silence she would have taken for maturity. His body was featureless, a bulk of darkness outlined by the fire's dark light.

Clara was laid off later that year. The entire night shift had been cut before she was let go, rumours had been circulating for weeks that more lay-offs were coming. Most people said there were less than five years left in the mine and then the whole thing would be shut down. The strike in '72 turned out to be the last protracted labour dispute at the Black Rock mine. All the Company needed, people said, was an excuse to pull out early and cut their losses and the union wasn't willing to provide one.

Clara decided to move into her grandmother's house near Harbour Grace which had been sitting empty since her death, and had been left to her by her father. Her mother drove up to help pack for the move. She sat with Jacob in her lap, running her fingers through his short brown hair. "What are you going to do for work out there?" she wanted to know. "Why don't you and Jake come stay with me?"

"I'll find something," Clara told her.

"It's Jacob you have to think about now," her mother said, "not yourself. What a single woman with a six year old is going to find out there I don't know. If you had gotten married to his father."

"Mom," Clara said, "we've been through this."

"Well, the boy needs a father," she said sternly. "He needs a family."

Clara slapped a handful of plates into a box. "And is that what you were thinking when you left, Betty? What about our family?"

Her mother stiffened in the chair, lifted Jacob off her lap and stood up. "I didn't leave until you and your brother were on your own," she said. "Until you had something for yourselves. It wasn't you two I walked out on." She moved her hands down her thighs to straighten her skirt and Clara thought she was about to leave, but her mother simply turned her back and began packing cookbooks into a box.

Clara had found an envelope among the few papers her father set aside before he died, sealed and addressed in his shaky handwriting: *To Betty.* When her mother opened it after the funeral she didn't say a word, didn't even remove the contents. She passed it to Clara and left the room for a long time. Inside the envelope was an airline ticket to Florida. Clara knew her mother was too stubborn to use it, that she'd worked too hard to find her own way out. And in that respect, at least, she was just like her daughter.

Jacob stood on a chair at the counter beside Clara. He was

industrious and competent in a childish way, taking exaggerated care with each glass as he wrapped it. She thought of how she had spent the first months of her pregnancy ignoring him, wishing he would disappear. That memory scraped at the delicate skin of tenderness she felt for him until it was raw, until it was almost a new thing altogether. He was singing quietly to himself and as she watched him Clara felt like a stranger walking out of darkness into the spare, comforting light of a fire. She reached out her hand, touching the bare nape of his neck as gently as she knew how.

CONTINENTAL DRIFT

Mid-summer, 1967. Overnight, on the lower end of Main Street where the road turns toward the bunkhouses and begins its run out of town, a fault the size of a tree trunk fissured open in the pavement. The Company sent a crew to repair the crack but the men were unable to shovel enough asphalt into the gap to fill it. Even when they reached shoulder deep into the darkness with their shovels they couldn't touch bottom. Over the course of a week, truckloads of sand were hauled in to backfill the hole, but the size of the opening increased daily as more and more of the pavement's surface cracked and fell into blackness. A drift from the earliest mine site to the north of Black Rock had been dug so close to the surface that the ground was shifting and collapsing into the vacant space beneath it. Each day a small crowd gathered to observe this peculiar turn of events and speculate on the fate of the road.

She remembers standing with her mother among the bystanders. She was wearing a yellow cotton dress with a small green bow at the front. She clasped her mother's ring finger with her free hand, twirling the loose gold wedding band. It was bright and hot. She held a Fudgsicle that was melting over her fist. The smell of asphalt and gasoline had spoiled her appetite for the ice cream and her mother reached down to take it from her. She opened her purse to rummage for a tissue, wiped her daughter's sticky fingers clean, then turned to continue a conversation with the woman beside her.

Left to herself, she wandered toward the pavement where workers stood with hands on their hips, or removed hard hats to scratch their sweaty heads. By the time her mother reached her she was near the lip of the hole, staring into a darkness that seemed to be bottomless.

On the way home she gripped her mother's hand so fiercely that the wedding ring pinched the woman's fingers. "Not so hard," her mother snapped. "I'm not going anywhere."

They flew back to Newfoundland for their wedding, catching an early morning flight out of Vancouver. She carried a camera bag and a *Cosmopolitan* magazine. There was a child in her belly the size of the nail on her baby finger, a blossoming star of flesh.

They crossed the coastline of Nova Scotia in the late afternoon, heading over the Atlantic toward Newfoundland, the jagged shoreline of red rock cliffs beneath them like the rough edge of a torn cloth. Hal watched through the tiny window. "Hard to believe that's where she all come apart," he said.

She turned her face toward him. "Which?"

"Europe and North America. Africa." He was pointing through the window with his finger. "Used to be one land mass until it split along fault lines and things started drifting apart. We cut up a big map in geography class one year and fit the continents together like a jigsaw puzzle."

She turned back to her magazine, flipping absently through the pages.

"The stars too," he added, as if she seemed insufficiently

impressed. "The whole universe is expanding. Everything moves away from everything else."

She watched Hal's face, the smooth unblemished skin marked by deep lines around his eyes and at the corners of his mouth that made it look as if he was still in the process of being assembled. At times she thought he was too young to understand anything of what she feels.

The evening of her first day home she heard her father rustling upstairs, footsteps and the scrape of boxes, cupboard doors. Her sisters had just left the house to see to their children, Hal was on his way to Grand Falls to spend time with family before the wedding. Her father came down into the living room carrying an armful of material, carefully, as if he had a baby swaddled in his arms.

"You'll want to be wearing this I guess," he said.

She pressed the palm of her hand to her mouth. A sharp stitch of anxiety creased her chest and she drew a quick painful breath around it. Neither of her sisters had been offered the dress and she'd never even considered that it would be given to her.

"Dad," she said through her fingers. "I can't."

Her father cleared his throat, but didn't look up from the white drift of cotton and silk in his arms. "Your mother would've wanted you to wear it," he said. "You'll have to get it taken in or some such thing, she was a little bigger around the waist. And a little smaller in other places." He smiled awkwardly, as if he'd accidentally touched her in an inappropriate way. "There's the ring too. You can try them both on if you like."

She was crying when he looked up at her and he cleared his throat again, then turned quickly to set the dress down on a chair. "Whenever you're ready," he said, and he stepped out the back door.

Through the living room window she could see his figure silhouetted by the deepening blue of twilight, the featureless shape of his body like the dark centre of a bruise. She thought of the summer nights they'd spent sitting out there when she was a girl, before she learned how to hurt him. He had put the constellations in their place for her, naming the carousel of stars circling Polaris: the Seven Sisters, Orion, the Big Dipper. She loved watching the massive confusion of light resolve into form under the direction of his hand. It was a comfort to know the stars had names, had stories of their own. It made them feel nearer, less aloof.

Virgo, her mother's sign. "She's watching over you," her father said. "You ever feel lonely, you just remember she's up there."

She could no longer picture her mother's face, remembered only a scatter of details, like the arbitrary points of light her father had sketched into Orion: crooked shoulders, knees, three stars for the belt, a bow and sword. She could make a nearly whole person of her mother from memory, but she had no idea how much of it was real, and how much was simply her imagination.

When her father worked the four to twelve shift she would sit outside alone or with her younger sisters, staring at the perfectly legible constellations while he moved through the shafts that spiralled beneath the town. She had always thought of the mine as a cold place and her father as a dim star of warmth in that darkness. She would close her eyes and imagine him beside her, the heat of the man, the humid new-potato smell of him that was as individual as a signature.

It hurts her to remember how close they'd been, and how she'd turned against him as she grew older. Her father had watched it happen, helplessly, and his helplessness was one more thing she held against him.

She was almost thirty-two when she first met Hal. He came to work at the club in Vancouver as a bouncer. It was as upscale a venue as she'd ever danced in: soft lighting, clean dressing rooms, faux finish on the walls. Hal was only twenty-four. He had a careful haircut and clean shaven face, a diffident, under-stated manner, all of which gave him the air of a young clergy-man. His accent was as thick as a slice of homemade bread.

"Whattaya at?" he greeted her when they were first intro-duced.

"You're a long way from home," she said.

"Grand Falls," he admitted, nodding his head.

"Black Rock," she responded.

Hal smiled more broadly than usual. "Used to go into Black Rock for hockey games when I was in high school." He leaned in close to her face. "Sure we're practically related," he said.

For months afterwards they maintained a friendly but professional relationship. He stood at the door of the bar and watched her, shaking his head in amusement when she did something particularly provocative or outrageous, wrapping her leg around the neck of a patron during a table dance, holding her face centimetres from the wide eyes of grey-haired men and whispering words they had never heard on the lips of a woman. She used to catch his eye, winking playfully in his direction, as if they were sharing a private joke. "Better go easy on them white heads," he warned her afterwards. "I don't know CPR."

When the easy banter ended, it ended suddenly. Hal began turning away from her, busying himself with his hands, adjusting his tie, running fingers through his immaculately combed hair. He greeted her with a clipped nod. Without reason or warning he seemed to have developed an intense dislike for her, for the way she made a living.

"Hey, Reverend," she said on her way out the door one evening, "if this kind of thing disgusts you, you should really get into another line of work."

He stared at her with a look full of dumb, animal sadness. She stopped and watched him for a moment, a certainty blossoming in the pit of her stomach, a feeling like standing at the lip of a precipice and looking down. Vertigo.

After his wife died, her father depended on his oldest daughter to read him stories from the paper, report cards and letters from his children's teachers. She can't remember exactly when it began to feel like a chore, then an embarrassment. As she moved through junior high school, her father's illiteracy grew in significance in her own mind. It became something she was ashamed of on his behalf, as if he regularly walked through town naked and was blissfully unaware of the fact.

It fell to her to help her sisters with their schooling. She cut the alphabet out of construction paper and taped the letters to the fridge, quizzing them both over breakfast. She thought it would be a simple thing to include her father in the process and she tried to involve him as casually as possible. Her sisters took turns identifying letters, then she would point to the A. *A is for apple,* she thought, trying to will the words into her father's mind. "Your turn, Dad," she offered cheerfully.

He looked up from his tea cup, a slice of half-soaked toast in his hand. "My lover," he said, laughing. "My poor little head is full."

It was simple obstinance on her father's part as far as she could see and she responded with obstinance of her own. She began making things up when she read him the specials at the local grocery store or program notes in the TV guide. "Bologna is on for fifteen cents a pound." " 'Sunday Night Wrestling' will be pre-empted by 'The Nature of Things.' " She started speaking to Sylvia and Leona in code, spelling out words she wanted to keep from his ears: names of boys she thought she might marry, talk about her periods and flatulence, her first experiences with sex. "H-a-n-d up my b-l-o-u-s-e," she said, loud enough to be overheard. Her sisters responding with appropriately scandalized whispers of "Holy s-h-i-t."

"Give up that foolishness," her father warned half-heartedly, but she carried on just to spite him. It made him seem oddly powerless, almost ridiculous, not to have mastered a thing as simple as reading and writing. She tried to remember what her world was like before she learned to read herself, but she could think of it only as a deformity, a kind of blindness, and she treated him with all the condescension she thought such a condition deserved. Everything she had once admired and loved in him she began to see as poor compensation for all that he lacked.

"Going out to the bridge for a smoke," he'd say as he pushed away from the supper table. "Anyone coming?"

She snorted uncomfortably, as if he'd asked her to join him in the bath. "No," she said with her face in her plate.

"Suit yourself," he said with a shrug. Mrs. Harris, who helped out at the house three days a week, tch tched under her breath and got up to clear dishes. Her sisters went to the door to pull on their sweaters.

"Beautiful night you're missing," her father said quietly.

She got up from the table and headed for the stairs. She was embarrassed to have denied him so publicly, and disguised it by being spiteful. "If you had a shower," she said on the way to her room, "I might consider it."

He wanted her to go to university in St. John's once she finished high school. "A girl with a head like yours should do something with it," he said.

"Don't go trying to live your life through me," she warned him.

She doesn't know how she learned these things, how she knew exactly what to say to hurt him most. It was like a facility for languages or math, coming to her easily and without conscious effort.

Hal came to her apartment with flowers. She was dressed in a t-shirt and black tights, her untidy hair pulled back with a barrette. "So how do you like the real me?" she asked.

"Well enough I guess," he said. He looked pained and embarrassed, as if she had recently caught him doing something he was ashamed of, as if she had walked in on him while he was masturbating. She took the bouquet from his arms and invited him in. "Selena's not my real name," she told him. She was setting the roses in a vase of water on the table beside the balcony door.

"Get away," Hal said sarcastically, as if she had confessed an infidelity he'd been aware of for years. He couldn't look at her, and stared instead at the arm of his sport jacket, picking imaginary lint from the material.

She felt incredibly tired, the afternoon light in the apartment hurt her eyes. She cupped her breasts in her hands and lifted them slightly, holding them as if they weren't a part of her body, as if she was testing the weight and freshness of fruit at the market. "I'm ready to give up this business," she said. She dropped her hands back to her sides. "If I thought I could make a living at something else, I'd be gone."

"I'm pulling a decent wage," Hal said.

She stared at his face, at the deep lines and the high red colour in his cheeks. "Well thank my lucky stars," she said. "Are you going to rescue a fallen woman Hal?"

"If that's what you want," he said stubbornly.

She sat in a wicker chair beside the table and hugged her knees. She couldn't stop thinking of his coldness toward her, how easily love can be mistaken for something else, for something almost exactly its opposite. She turned to look at the flowers on the table beside her, the thick fragrance like an invisible halo around their dark heads. "Florence," she said then, in a tone that was almost accusatory.

He looked at her, uncomprehending. "Florence," he repeated stupidly, as if speaking the word would unlock its meaning.

"That's my name," she said. "Florence."

He shrugged. "I could get used to that," he said.

She had always envied her younger sisters: their uncomplicated desires, their lives following an ordered predictable path. They had always let her set the limits and then watched her break them, simultaneously scandalized and relieved by her behaviour. Two years after finishing high school she moved to British Columbia. That was just like Florence, her sisters said. Not just leaving, but going as far as the country allowed. After that break, they both felt they had no choice but to stay behind in Black Rock, to marry local boys, to keep their father company.

Her occupation was another thing. She had always assumed it would follow a slow descent into desperate poverty and drugs, or extortion at the hands of a ruthless man, but in her case it was a practical decision. She was tired of scraping by as a waitress and the ready money was too good to turn down. She hadn't intended it to go on longer than a few months, and she thought of herself as *between jobs* for years. Even after she reconciled herself to her position, she realized she could never admit it to her father. And she knew this secret would come between them as well.

She remembers spelling it out to her sisters in the kitchen during a visit home, how they were shocked in a pleased sort of way. "Holy s-h-i-t," they repeated under their breath.

"Healthy r-e-m-u-n-e-r-a-t-i-o-n," Florence defended herself. "I'm not a-s-h-a-m-e-d of my b-o-d-y."

Her father listening to them from the living room. "What?" he shouted. "What are you bunch going on about now?"

She assumes it got back to him eventually. She could feel the growing strain of avoiding the subject in their telephone conversations, as if the ends of the continent were drifting away from each other and their voices had to carry further and further every time they spoke.

The priest smiled towards them as she and her father walked the narrow carpeted aisle to the altar. Her father wore a dark blue pin stripe suit, his hair awkwardly slicked back from his forehead. Wafts of after-shave rose from his face like heat over pavement. Florence wore her mother's wedding gown.

She knows her father meant the dress to bring them together again, all three of them, as if the life they'd shared could be restored that simply: taken in, hemmed, tucked and drycleaned. As if the separate worlds they had come to occupy could be snapped neatly into place like pieces of a puzzle.

At her mother's funeral, when he lifted Florence up at the coffin, she'd gripped the sleeve of her mother's dress and wouldn't let go. Her father pried her fingers loose and carried her away in tears. "You hurt me," she shouted at him, "You hurt my hand!" She cupped it in her lap and cried helplessly, relieved to have a pain to root her grief, to give it a shape she could articulate.

"Who gives this woman away?" the priest asked with a look of beatific boredom. Her father raised his hand, whispered a hoarse "I do," then stepped away to his seat.

She stood alone beside Hal then, and she watched his face

from the corner of her eye. She could see what he was thinking: their whole lives ahead of them, the child. Love, she
thought as she watched her mother's wedding band slip onto
her finger, love makes life no easier. And it was as much as a
person could hope for.

The first time she felt the baby move she and Hal were on the
ferry coming back from a Saturday in Victoria. They stood
against the railing, watching the lights of the city burning like a
field of stars in the distance, the constellations of the night sky
dimmed by their brightness. It was a turning inside her body she
felt, that first movement away from her. She grabbed Hal's arm
above the elbow, holding her free hand against her belly.

"What is it," Hal asked. "Are you going to be sick?"

She moved her hands back to the railing and shook her
head no. The hair bristled stiffly along the length of her arms.
It was a terrifying confirmation, the baby discovering movement, agency. There was another creature alive inside her.

After its single subtle announcement the child lay still. She
found herself selfishly wishing she could go on carrying it in
the veined nest of her womb, feeding it with her own life,
never letting go. She looked up at the sky, turning to search
among the dim stars, and she felt the sideways tug of vertigo,
her hand reaching for something to steady herself. Hal gripped
her elbow. "What is it?" he asked, craning his neck to stare
upward in the same direction.

"Virgo," she said, pointing.

It was moving steadily away from them.

SKIN

The sky was heavy and grey with cloud. A dull, grainy drizzle gave the whole town the feel of an old black-and-white photograph. Austin gestured toward his old hangouts as the wedding cavalcade meandered through town littering the streets with tissue paper flowers. There was Wong's restaurant (pinball, learning to swear), the Lion's Club playground (pissing contests, first kiss), the outdoor swimming pool (first sight of a naked breast). "Spare me the details," Melinda said at that point, throwing up her hands.

From the look of it, the pool had been closed for years, strips of the green plastic torn away from the wire fencing, the dressing rooms unpainted and dilapidated. Austin was surprised by how small everything felt, by the number of buildings that had disappeared since the mine closed, the Company bunkhouses torn down, the old store-house behind the pool gone too.

"What did you expect?" Melinda wanted to know. "It's been fifteen years."

Austin shrugged helplessly, feeling misunderstood. "I just didn't expect everything to be different. I wouldn't have recognized Batman if he pissed on my shoes."

"He grew up Austin. How long did you think he'd go around being called *Batman*?"

The simple matter-of-factness in her voice irked him. He shrugged again. "I guess," he said. "I'll never get used to calling him *Gerald* though. Gerald," he repeated. "I haven't called him that since he climbed into the rafters at the pool to watch the girls change."

Melinda shook her head. "Bit of a horny prick, that friend of yours."

Austin looked across at her, his face puckered sourly. Melinda turned her attention to his hands on the steering wheel, reaching out to brush her fingers against the bracelet of fine red hair at his wrist. There was nothing apologetic in the gesture. It was simple consolation, as if she was trying to comfort a child with a toothache.

At the Union Hall they sat through a meal of roast beef and soggy mashed potatoes and half an hour of barely audible speeches. Afterwards, tables were pushed back against the walls and the lights were turned down for the dance. A woman in a pink blouse approached their table: curly brown hair pulled back with a scrunchy; the stout belly he had lain on. "Roberta," he said.

"Roberta," she repeated to Melinda, introducing herself. "The wife?"

Melinda tipped her head slightly from side to side, as if she was trying something on for size before a mirror. "More or less," she decided.

"Mind if I take him up for a dance?"

"I'm not much of a dancer," Austin protested.

"Go on," Melinda said. "He loves to dance," she told Roberta. "Go on."

The dance floor was crowded, there were balloons and streamers hanging so low overhead that they touched the hair of the tallest dancers. The song ended suddenly, a waltz began, and Roberta moved into Austin's body without hesitating, stretching to reach her arms around his neck. She looked up at him with a wide, brazen smile. It was the same careless assurance she'd shown him the last time he'd seen her, just days before he left Black Rock for good.

It was a warm evening in June, threatening rain. He and Batman and Roberta passed each beer between them, and Roberta, who was a year older than the boys, guzzled three or four mouthfuls at a go. Batman looked at Austin and smiled as she drank. Austin touched his chest with his index finger. *Me first.* Batman patted his back pocket where he carried the safes.

Roberta was doing most of the drinking, but halfway through the case both Austin and Batman were laughing stupidly. Batman got up to take a piss and fell sideways like a tree sawn off at the base, then crawled giggling into the bushes.

"Open us another one," Roberta said to Austin, showing him the empty bottle. She was peeling the label off, being careful not to rip it. Austin took the cap off a full beer with a satisfying pop and Roberta stuck a finger in her cheek, imitating the sound. He passed her the bottle. Roberta got up from her rock to sit beside him. She put a hand on his leg and he looked down at her fingers, a gold ring on each, a slave ring on the thumb. He wondered what the hell was taking Batman so long. "You shouldn't have to leave town a virgin," she told him.

"I'm not a virgin," he lied.

"Whatever," Roberta said. She put her hand on the crotch of his jeans and kissed him, her tongue exploring his mouth with the confidence of an animal sniffing a younger, smaller animal. He could taste the beer, a stale undertone of spearmint gum. Then Roberta stood up and walked toward a group of pine trees, undoing the snap of her jeans as she went, pulling them down as she settled on the grass. It was nearly dark now, but Austin could make out the pale white of her thighs when she lay back, the brown patch of pubic hair at her crotch. "Put it on," she whispered as he scrambled in beside her.

"What?"

"The safe," she said. "Put it on."

Austin knelt beside her in silence for a moment. "Batman has them."

"Jesus Christ," Roberta said, sitting up. "Batman," she shouted into the darkness. "Bring over the frigging safes."

Austin lay back and waited. He could hear the wind moving in the trees overhead and the sound of Batman stumbling towards them through the bushes, and Roberta sat beside him naked below the waist.

He stood almost a foot taller than her now. He stared over her head at a point in the distance, avoiding her face.

"How long you two been together?" Roberta asked him.

"Two years, give or take."

"She's not bad looking," Roberta told him. "You did all right for yourself, I'd say." Austin nodded his head. He placed his hands carefully on Roberta's back and didn't move them through the entire song.

"Who was that?" Melinda asked when he'd made his way back to the table.

"Someone I knew from school." He grabbed a handful of peanuts and tried to smile across at her. Melinda pursed her lips into a frown, but let it drop. Austin's palms were wet with sweat, the pit of his stomach lurched and balled, lurched and balled. It was a ridiculous, unnecessary deceit. He didn't understand what he was hiding from her or why he'd lied to her in the first place.

They'd just moved into the apartment on Gower St. There were no curtains on the windows, everything they owned was still in boxes. They ate Kraft Dinner from the pot, drank red wine out of dusty Coca-Cola glasses to celebrate the occasion, and as it was getting dark they made love on the box-spring mattress, the bed frame lying in pieces beside them on the floor. When she moved to take him into her mouth Austin stopped her. He lay along the naked length of her body, entering her almost involuntarily when she opened her legs beneath him.

It had taken Melinda months to convince Austin to try much of anything beyond the missionary position when they first began having sex. "Old Faithful," she liked to call it. Austin could tell she was making fun of him, but the spiritual connotations appealed to him. He wanted to see her face while he was inside her, to look into her eyes when he came.

They made love quietly and held each other for a long time afterwards, Austin cupping the swell of Melinda's belly in his hand, his thumb fitting perfectly over the small depression of her navel. The room was dark except for the silver glow of a streetlamp outside the window. He was almost asleep when Melinda rolled to face him, kissing him on the chin. "Hey," he murmured sleepily, pressing his mouth to her forehead. "Austin," she said, "how did you lose your virginity?"

He lay suddenly still and alert, and then moved away from her to sit back against the wall. A slick film of perspiration formed on his palms.

"I'll tell you my story first if you like," Melinda offered, trying to soothe his obvious discomfort.

"Alright," he said without relief, "you first."

Melinda straightened her pillow to sit back against the wall beside him, her knees drawn up under the sheets, her slender face divided neatly into light and shadow. She'd just turned seventeen and was saying goodnight to her boyfriend. They did it standing up in her porch while her parents watched a rerun of "Perry Mason" in the living room, her face against the cold wood of the door, her feet balanced on winter boots and shoes. "It hurt a little," she said, "in a strange way. It was a kind of hurt I knew I'd never feel again." She told him about reaching behind to touch her boyfriend's softening cock, the skin slippery with wetness. Austin listened in silence, feeling slightly lost, unsure what she wanted him to do with this information. Melinda turned on the bed then and reached down across his belly under the sheet, her hand moving to his flaccid penis, then quickly back to his stomach. "Your turn," she said quietly.

Austin told her about a girl he'd dated when he was sixteen. She was in his Grade Nine class, they had been seeing one another for months by then. She was wearing a yellow terry-cloth tank top and shorts and white ankle socks that she didn't take off. She put a scratchy copy of Fleetwood Mac's "Rumours" on the stereo in Austin's bedroom and before the end of side one it was all over.

What he didn't tell Melinda about was the night down by the Mudhole, the grass burns on his bare knees and Roberta's soft belly beneath him. He didn't say anything about rolling off her into the grass and throwing up, about stumbling home and sleeping with all his clothes on, about finding the soiled condom, like a dried placenta, still clinging to his cock the next morning. He hadn't seen or talked to Roberta since. *Skin*, they called it back then, *a piece of skin*.

He watched Melinda across the table, her blonde head perched on the slender stem of her neck. There was such a misleading air of fragility about her. She reached for her glass of rye and Coke. "What is it?" she asked, catching his stare.

"Nothing. Your drink ok?" He didn't understand why he felt so ridiculously guilty when she was the one who'd been unfaithful.

The groom staggered to their table. His shoulder-length hair curled up at the bottom like the pages of a paperback left out in humid weather, tiny rivulets of sweat ran down his face and disappeared into his carefully clipped goatee. The doors at both ends of the hall were propped open with chairs, the room sticky with the heat of the crowd. "I see," Gerald said to Austin loudly, "that Berta got her paws on you already. Better keep an eye on them two," he warned Melinda with a wink.

"Gerald," Austin said testily, staring at the table.

"Fuck off, *Gerald*. That's Batman to you buddy."

Austin lifted his drink, draining the glass, smiling in spite of himself.

"She's married too now. Got three kids of her own. Oldest almost eleven I'd say."

"What are you and the missus going to do now?" Austin asked him, trying to change the subject. "Staying around here?"

Gerald shrugged. "Where've I got to go?" He looked into

his nearly empty glass. "Want one?" he asked, already on the way to the bar.

For the rest of the evening Melinda didn't ask any questions about Roberta or Austin's connection to her although he felt them, the way an animal can sense rain in the air hours before it arrives. He wondered what she was thinking, whether she was the slightest bit jealous. He thought of how matter-of-factly she'd confessed to sleeping with Phil Hanrahan, her head against the bare skin of Austin's chest. His heartbeat was like a tiny fist slapping her cheek. She looked up at him, the blood vessels below the pale skin of his face becoming brighter, more prominent, like a slide under a microscope coming into focus.

"Why are you telling me this?" he asked her.

"I wanted you to know. I thought you deserved to know."

"Well thank you very much," Austin said as he pushed away from her and out of bed, "for considering my feelings."

"Austin," she said. "He doesn't mean anything to me."

"Spare me the details. Alright?" He was pacing naked beside the bed, his penis flapping against his thighs, too furious to care how ridiculous he looked. He went to the closet and pulled out a suitcase, opening it on the bed.

"Don't be stupid Austin," Melinda said. She got up and began returning his clothes to the drawers as he continued trying to fill the suitcase. They carried on like this for several minutes, two naked adults, one packing, the other emptying an open suitcase.

"Fuck off," Austin said. "Leave me alone."

He packed the same shirt three times, the same handful of underwear. Sleet smacked the window pane. Finally Austin sat on the floor and wept. Melinda, who was crying too by this point, pulled on her bathrobe and went to the kitchen to make tea.

Through the spring and summer they ran through variations of the exact same conversation a hundred times, the heat slowly dissipating from their arguments so that it sometimes seemed they were discussing the experience of another couple altogether.

On the night before they drove into Black Rock for the wedding Austin pulled the suitcase out of the closet again.

"Why does everything come down to sex for you?" she asked him.

Austin stopped to look at her, a pair of blue underwear in his hand as if he was offering it to her. "If you want my opinion," he said in the same measured, reasonable tone, "that's a question you should ask yourself, not me."

Melinda took the underwear from him, folding it neatly on his side of the suitcase. She reached out and grabbed his jeans by the waist, pulling him close to her. "Please," she whispered. "Austin. You're going to have to get past this."

"I can't," he said, turning away to the chest of drawers, pulling out more underwear, socks.

She sat on the bed beside the suitcase. "You're going to have to get past this," she said again.

After most of the guests had left the Hall for the night, after she'd had half a dozen drinks, Melinda dragged Austin onto the dance floor for a waltz. He was too drunk himself to offer much resistance. He felt the contours of her body against his, her breasts, her belly and hips moving against him, her head in the crook of his neck. More than anything at that moment he wanted to kiss her, to touch every inch of her skin with his mouth. But he placed his hands carefully on her back and didn't move them through the entire song.

It was after two in the morning by the time they decided to call it quits. "We better leave the car," Melinda suggested, and they walked in silence across town, past the pool, the playground, the restaurant. The sky had cleared and there was a nearly full moon lighting the streets. A cool breeze lifted the sweat-soaked clothing from their skin in gusts. At the bed and breakfast they undressed and climbed into bed together, the moon shadowing the room through the window, the bed sheets, their clothes, the furniture lying in shades of silver, grey and black. They lay side by side without speaking for a long time and then Melinda reached a hand across to touch him, her fingernails circling the smooth hairless skin at his hip. "You don't have to tell me if you don't want to," she said.

Austin looked at her quickly, then turned away: he had been thinking about Roberta too, imagining her with her husband, holding his bare thighs to move him deeper inside her when they fucked. That gesture of devotion or moderate affection or simple lust, he couldn't understand how people held those strands separately in their heads. Melinda's hand strayed across Austin's naked belly and he turned toward her, his mouth finding her shoulder in the darkness. She moved him above her, reaching her hand down to place his half-erect penis inside her. "Old faithful," she whispered into his ear.

It had been months since they made love and it felt strange to Austin to come back to it now, as if it was something different from what he expected, something smaller. He rolled away from Melinda onto his back and lifted her over his hips so he could see her face in the light of the moon outside, her eyes closed, her lips pursed slightly as she reached down and took him inside her again. He thought of her moving this way with Phil Hanrahan, with a dozen other men for all he knew, and at that moment it didn't seem to matter to him in the least.

MIRACLES

For convenience sake, let's say this story begins on a clear night in October. The moon is full, it stands out against the darkness like a single braille dot perforated on a black page. If you could reach your hand up to touch the sky, you would feel it raised beneath your skin like the improbable beginning of a letter, a word, another story. The air is cool, the leaves on all the trees have turned and started falling; they make an ambiguous rustle as you walk through their brittle brilliance, rich and melancholy all at once.

My brother and his wife are celebrating their tenth anniversary. I've been invited to join them for dinner, and after repeated attempts to shirk the obligation, I have relented. I don't enjoy the walk across town. I don't notice the moon, or the cool air except to pull my coat tight at the collar. I have a small package of fresh mussels under my arm—a surprise— my contribution to the evening meal. When I reach their house I stand at the front door for a moment, as if even now I might change my mind. It's been so long since I've visited that I feel compelled to knock and wait for permission to enter.

My younger brother answers the door and takes my coat; his wife, Jade, offers me a drink. We make stilted small talk about the weather, the state of things at the mine while Jade steams the mussels and then we sit at the table to eat. My brother stabs a mussel with his fork, eats it, reaches for another.

"Are you sure you should do that, Kim?" Jade asks him.

That's my brother's name, Kim. A peculiar name for a boy, and even more peculiar at the time he was born, in a small community in Newfoundland. If I want to be honest, I'd have to say that's where our problems began, his name. And now that I think about it, maybe that's where I should have begun.

Mother had always warned us about the danger of putting convenience ahead of other things, like truth for instance, or thoroughness, which in her mind were almost synonymous. She was a strict Salvation Army woman, our mother, and though Father attended church only for baptisms, weddings and funerals, Mother marched into her uniform every Sunday. Morning and evening she took her black leather Bible and silver trumpet from a shelf in the back porch and headed off to the Salvation Army Hall without him.

She had a no-nonsense approach to her religion that some servants of the obvious would label "military," but might more properly be called rigorous. Practical. She was always raising money for an overseas mission, or an alcohol treatment program, or a Christmas soup kitchen. Mother was also a member of the infamous Salvation Army band that commandeered the busiest corner of Black Rock's Main Street every Saturday in December and honked out metallic renditions of Christmas carols for most of the afternoon.

She loved to sing old hymns as she worked around the house as well, "Onward, Christian Soldiers" being her favourite. It was a kind of battle cry against "domestic ungodliness." When she was called upon to break up a wrestling match between myself and Kim, twisting an ear on each head to keep us apart, you could sometimes hear her humming the refrain under her breath. One Sunday after-noon she brought out the trumpet and played it for fifteen minutes in the kitchen because Father had the unmitigated gall to sit down to a game of cards on the Seventh Day. He gave up on it finally, knowing Mother would go on till her lips fell off if he persisted.

But I was speaking about my brother's name. I was only a year old when Kim was born and it was a long time before I realized how strange a name it was and began asking questions. The story goes that in the third month of her second pregnancy my mother had a dream. And in the dream an angel of the Lord appeared unto her and announced she was going to give birth to a girl-child whose name was to be Kimberly. Mother put little stock in dreams and not much more in angels, and the anointed name was so ridiculous that she put the whole episode down to the pickled eggs she'd been eating by the dozen. But such a visitation was so alien to her tradition, so foreign and unexpected, that she was unable to dismiss it com-pletely. Days before she delivered she had the dream a second time and Mother resolved to act in accordance with what she saw as the Will of God.

"But he wasn't a girl," I pointed out.

"Yes, well," Mother said. "There was some kind of mix up I suppose."

Father expressed his misgivings about the name after the birth and even Mother was perplexed by this turn of events. Still, she decided to shorten the name from Kimberly to "Kim" and go ahead with the christening. My father, having voiced his objections, wouldn't stand in the way of what he called her "religious convictions."

As far as I know nothing came of it. No descending doves, no parted waters, no speaking in tongues. I was the one who attended church regularly with Mother, and kept her company outside the Imperial General Store on bitter winter evenings before Christmas with a bell and the Salvation Army donation bubble. I was the one who wanted my own uniform and black leather Bible, who joined the junior band and tried desperately to learn how to play something, descending inexorably from trumpet to tuba to bass drum to the lowly tambourine.

"Mother," I said to her during the walk home from church one Sunday morning, "did you ever have any dreams about me?"

She looked sideways in my direction. It was a hot August morning, there were lines of perspiration trickling from beneath the band of her officer's cap. I felt embarrassed to have asked, but plowed stubbornly ahead. "Before I was born, I mean," I clarified.

"Why yes, of course," she said. Her tone was cheerful but she looked uncertain, as if God was late with a sign she'd been promised. "Haven't I ever told you? Well," she said, "I had this dream three times before you were born. I was asleep in my bed and the angel of the Lord appeared unto me. It was so bright, Stuart, that it hurt my eyes. It was as if the room was on fire. And then the angel spoke without moving its mouth. This voice seemed to come from all around me, from the air. 'You are going to have a son' the voice said. . . ."

"Didn't the angel say 'boy-child'?" I interrupted.

"Yes, you're quite right, now that I think about it, that was what the angel said. 'You are going to have a boy-child,' it said, 'and you shall name him Stuart.'"

"But I thought I was named after Poppy Ellsworth," I said suspiciously.

"Why yes," Mother said, hesitating a little. She took a tissue from her purse and mopped her brow. "That too," she said.

Our house on Pine Street was identical to the other Company houses in design, but the details reflected my parents: family pictures, sturdy furniture, basic colours, nothing garish or flashy or outrageous. They even managed to avoid the sparkled stucco craze that gripped the town during the early seventies, sticking resolutely to flat white ceilings. In many ways, Mother and Father were remarkably similar people: serious, stubborn, straightforward.

There was a lot of talk about Saving in that house. Father grew up during the Depression and never fully recovered from the experience. His next meal wasn't something he ever learned to take for granted. He was happiest sitting down with his blue bank book to go through each entry, adding and subtracting meticulously on a piece of scrap paper. The result was never in question, he just enjoyed the confirmation, the sense of security it gave him, however brief.

My mother *tch tched* over this obsession of his. "You can't take it with you, Father," she'd tell him. Mother was more concerned with saving souls than money. Though that's too strong a word I think. "Soul" was too airy-fairy for Mother, not concrete enough, not at all practical. She preferred to use "person" or "individual"; to her mind they were more inclusive, they didn't over-simplify.

"Father," she might announce as she came through the

front door after a Sunday service, "an individual was saved this morning!"

"Praise be," Father would say over the potatoes and carrots he was peeling for Sunday dinner, and he said it without a trace of irony. He was never fierce in his disbelief, or evangelical about it, he simply hadn't managed to settle anything to his own satisfaction.

Throughout our childhood and adolescence Kim and I fell on either side of that issue like opposite sides of a coin. Our parents never pressured us either way, but being young and being brothers, we weren't as kind to each other. He ridiculed my earnest fundamentalism. I badgered him to come out to church, to the youth group. These encounters usually ended in physical confrontations that Mother was forced to break up with our ears twisted in her fingers and a hymn barely audible on her breath.

By the age of fourteen I had become passionately interested in miracles. Having read through the entire Bible, and the Gospels twice, I was struck by the kinds of stories that were rarely mentioned at the Salvation Army Hall, or were glossed over briefly at best. Sermons and studies tended to focus on the Good Samaritan approach, the Boy Scoutish good-deed-a-day variety of religion. I was fascinated by the inexplicable, by the way Spirit transformed the physical, imbued it with properties it had lost or never possessed: the voice in the burning bush, the feeding of the five thousand, the healing of the blind and the cleansing of lepers. That spark lurked in the cells of all things like a dormant seed, a knot of latent potential.

This passion caused my mother some concern. She'd been brought up to think of miracles as a *Catholic thing*, a questionable devotion to pictures of the Madonna that wept real tears, and her own ambiguous experience with the "angel of the Lord" made her wary. She *tch tched* over it in the same resigned tone that she used for Father and his bank book.

It was Kim who was most offended by my obsession. His doubts about spiritual matters were confirmed in his Grade Seven science class where they were studying evolution. He began tracing caricatures of apes and tacking them to my door, leaving them on my desk, taping them to the bathroom mirror when I showered. *Stuart,* he scribbled across the top of each drawing, *the one that got left behind.*

I suppose I was an embarrassment to him. He was one of the best players on the local bantam hockey team. He pursued his burgeoning interest in girls with the same adolescent fervour I brought to my faith. He wanted an older brother he could look up to publicly, someone who could fight or smoked cigarettes behind the school. All I offered were lectures on "healing prayer" and "life after death" and inept tambourine lessons. It was Kim's popularity that protected me from the worst of the persecution I might have received from other kids and he probably resented that fact. Even if he had wanted to love me then, I made it impossible.

One Saturday morning the summer I turned sixteen, I was pulled out of sleep by the Company siren. ASAMCo provided fire-fighting services for the community and everyone knew the sector codes—one blast meant fire on Company property; two was the north end, from Main Street across to the post office; three was our side of town, from Main Street to Pine;

and four meant the townsite to the north of Company housing. As I scrambled downstairs in my underwear that morning the prospect of disaster set my body vibrating like a struck bell. I'd never heard anything like this before, the siren went on and on in the grey dawn light.

Mother was standing at the window in her housecoat. Father was already dressed and pulling on his work boots, tying the laces with methodical fierceness.

"What is it?" I asked.

Father didn't look up. Mother held her hand to her mouth as if she were about to cry. Kim came into the kitchen behind me, still half asleep. "What is it?" he said.

We hardly saw Father over the next three days. He'd come home at odd hours, sleep for an hour or two and then head back to the mine. No one in town slept much more than that. The rock had fallen in the Number 7 shaft of the old Lucky Strike mine and seven men were under.

The churches organized a constant prayer vigil, and there was an ecumenical service at the Roman Catholic church, the largest in Black Rock. I spent a lot of time in those three days on my knees. It was the first time I had a concern I felt was worthy of the grand gesture. I don't know what I wanted exactly. Proof I guess, a sign that God was acting in our lives in some tangible, quantifiable way. Something that Kim couldn't refute.

They made it through late on the third day, and six of the men were found alive. The seventh, Clay Keough, had been killed under the fall of stone. He was only a year away from retirement.

"Well," Mother said, "thank God the other six came out alive."

"Not much consolation to old Clay probably," Father said, and that's where they left it.

Kim had dismissed my requests for divine intervention from the start, and he taunted me with the dead man, held up the corpse the way some preachers hold up the Gospel, as if it were ultimate and indisputable truth. There were a thousand things I could have said to him, I could have talked about the unfathomable Will of God, I could have said something about faith and the lack of it. *Where wast thou,* I could have quoted, *when I laid the foundations of the earth?* But Clayton was dead for all that.

"It could've been Father down there," Kim shouted at me. The slight, almost pretty features of his face had the ruthless focus of a predator on the scent of blood. "They could both die tomorrow," he said.

Things seem completely inevitable in retrospect. Even though it took place two years later after countless ordinary events, after thousands of inconsequential moments, it seemed to me that the next piece of this story—the hardest part—was set in motion and followed inexorably from that time, from those arguments.

It was a clear night in October. I was supervising a youth group sleep-over at the Army hall, Kim was away at a weekend hockey tournament in Corner Brook. I'd managed to settle everyone into their sleeping bags with the usual combination of empty threats and pleading, and had just begun drifting off when the siren began wailing. One. Two. Three. "Stuart," one of the kids whispered in the darkness, "that's your side of town."

They tell me my parents died in their beds, of smoke inhalation, before the flames touched them. An investigation placed the blame on faulty wiring and speculated that the fire may have smouldered behind the wall for days before erupting into the living room. By the time I reached the house that night the entire quad was burning. A helpless audience of neighbours stood about in nightgowns and undershirts. The light of the fire gave the street an intense, subterranean glow that made it seem as if the event was taking place underground. As if the entire town had been swallowed by grief.

The next September Kim left for university in St. John's. I was hired on as a clerk at the Company office and eventually worked my way up to accountant, taking night courses at the public school. I lived alone in a Company apartment and kept to myself. I stopped attending church, and as much as possible in a town the size of Black Rock, I avoided the people I'd grown up with at the Salvation Army Hall. My days were devoted to the artless certainties of arithmetic, my evenings to the television's bland menu of black-and-white movies and hokey Hollywood biblical epics.

In St. John's, Kim fell in love with Jade, a Fine Arts student who had come to Newfoundland from New York to study after she'd read *Death on the Ice*. She thought it would bring her closer to a world where nature still reigned, like Job's God, both provident and pitiless. She was disappointed to find herself in a real city, a small one granted, but a city nonetheless, with cinemas, theatres, public transit. Her only real consolation, she claims, was meeting Kim.

At their wedding Kim wore a traditional tuxedo, while Jade was adorned in a paper gown hand-sewn from the love letters she and Kim had written one another in the previous two years. "I know he doesn't seem like my type," I overheard her explaining to a friend from New York. "If it hadn't been for his name, I wouldn't have looked at him twice."

After he completed his engineering degree, Kim moved back to Black Rock where he worked with a team of prospectors, searching for a new mineral strike that would save the local industry from collapse. He made periodic attempts to establish a relationship with me but I kept him at a distance. Kim had never meant his ape caricatures as prophecy, I'm sure, but there I sat in the grey television light night after night: sullen, hopeless, deficient in some significant way. The One That Got Left Behind.

"Are you sure you should do that, Kim?" Jade asked my brother.

I looked at her quickly, then turned to Kim. "Is there something wrong with the mussels?"

"No no," Kim said. "It's me."

"The last time he ate mussels," Jade explained, "he had an allergic reaction."

"Don't make it sound so dramatic. I got a tickle in my throat, that's all. And it's worth it. These are great Stuart." He stabbed another one with his fork, knowing I would have been uncomfortable if he didn't touch them at all.

"I don't think it would be a good idea to eat any more," Jade said. There was an abrasive note of warning in her voice, like grains of broken glass in the fibres of a carpet, and Kim held up his hands in mock-surrender. "Alright," he managed as he chewed.

After the meal, we moved into the living room and sat with liqueurs. The conversation lurched uncomfortably as it had for most of the evening. Jade began presenting some of her latest sculptures and paintings and I tried to humour them both by paying attention.

"I'm trying to connect with something here," she said, holding a canvas upright on the floor. "Something at the core of things. I don't know if I've got it yet." There was a gnarled leafless tree against a background that might have been the barrens around Black Rock. The tree was in the approximate form of a cross. The piece was called "Salvation Landscape III."

Kim cleared his throat loudly and sipped his liqueur. "That's one of my favorites," he said to Jade. "I think you've really hit something there."

I stared at him in surprise. "That sounds a bit too flakey to come from you," I said, a little unkindly.

Kim shrugged, as if the abuse wasn't out of order. "Who knows, maybe she'll make a religious man out of me yet." He cleared his throat again. "There's that tickle," he said.

Jade scowled at him. "You know better," she said and got up to start clearing dishes from the table. Both Kim and I moved to help her but she waved us back into our chairs. Kim smiled at me through his obvious discomfort. "She's as stubborn as Mother," he said.

We sat in almost complete silence then, except for the clatter of Jade stacking dishes and the frequent sound of Kim clearing his throat. And as I stared at his reddening face, at his helplessly watering eyes, my grey, abysmal life unexpectedly erupted. It came to me like a vision, I saw it happening this way: the muscles at the back of Kim's throat swelling so severely that his windpipe was blocked, his body going into shock, convulsions. My brother, who had been right about the world all along, dead on the floor of his living room, a glass of Creme de Menthe spilled on the carpet.

It was as if a fire smouldering in the walls of a home had finally surfaced. "Jade," I shouted, my voice constricted to an octave above its natural range. "Jade, come in here."

Kim waved at me in annoyance, as if he was trying to quiet a child. "I'm alright," he said. "I'll be fine."

This story ends with the dream I had the night my brother and his wife celebrated their tenth anniversary, the night my brother said he would be fine and it was so, a clear night in October. There was a full moon, it stood out against the darkness like a single braille dot perforated on a black page. The leaves on all the trees had turned a brilliant red and were falling. All the way home I was shaking, pricked by this revelation, aware for the first time that what I wanted more than anything in the world was my brother to go on living. And to be there with him. Living.

I woke up in the old house on Pine Street. The rooms were full of light, luminous, as if the sun was out on all sides of the house at once. Downstairs I found Father in the kitchen, peeling a sinkful of potatoes and carrots for dinner. Sunday morning. I could hear the knife shearing the wet brown skins from the potatoes, and the serene tick of the stove clock. I don't think I was there as myself, in this body. Father took no notice of me and I didn't try to speak. I felt transparent and dispersed, like the air. There was a loud tramping on the step, and

Mother marched in through the front door in her uniform, holding the gleam of her silver trumpet.

"Father," she said triumphantly, "an individual was saved today!"

And my father looked up from the vegetables with a smile.

"Praise be," he said.

WHAT POSSESSED HIM

Hayward sat on the bed in the dark to catch his breath, to ease the ache in his chest after climbing the stairs. Through the window he could see the illuminated star on the steeple of the Anglican church two blocks away, the dark glow of light through stained glass on either side of the doors.

He heard his wife's voice. "Your shoes," she was saying. She was speaking from the foot of the stair. "Your shoes are on the stand. In the closet."

"I know where the shoes are," he shouted back, not angry, but louder than he needed to be heard.

From where he was sitting he still expected to look out on the Catholic school: the long line of classroom windows, the Blessed Virgin on a pedestal at the entrance with her hands held out in perpetual benediction. *Intercession*, Etta once corrected him. She'd gone steady with a Catholic boy before Hayward met her and had retained a great deal of the arcane knowledge he'd passed on. *Mary intercedes, she doesn't bless.* Hayward hadn't paid particular attention to what she was telling him and couldn't remember now what the distinction meant. He couldn't remember the name of the Catholic boy he'd replaced or what might have become of him. He stared across at the church in the distance, the newly-empty lot between graded level under snow. The view frightened him, made him feel displaced in his life. It was like a disfigurement of his own face, like seeing himself missing an eye.

He'd sat in the backyard for days that fall, watching the building come down. Not enough children in town to fill the classes of two institutions, the students amalgamated at the public school. A few Catholic parents protested briefly when these plans were announced, but there was no arguing with the reality of the situation. The roof came off first, followed by the white shingles, the rotten tarpaper. The boards underneath darkened by age, by insidious water damage. The building like a creature suffering through vivisection, stripped back a layer at a time to salvage windows, steel girders from the auditorium.

The day after they'd seen the specialist in Grand Falls, Etta came outside to stand beside him awhile. An afternoon too cold to be sitting in the yard without a hat, she told him. "You'll catch your death," she said.

Hayward was sitting in a lawn chair, his shoes buried in leaves fallen from the single birch tree in the yard. Mid-November, the snow late this year. "I've already caught that," he said.

Etta put her hand to her mouth then, staring at the mutilated school, a film of tears blurring the clear blue of her eyes.

Across the street a crane was lifting the statue of the Virgin Mary onto a flatbed truck. A saw started up somewhere out of view, ripping into the naked frame of the building. He could feel the noise shaking through the ground, travelling up through his spine.

She said, "You have to tell the boys, Hayward."

"Etta."

"They have a right to know."

He nodded. "Let them have one more Christmas," he'd said.

———————

The "boys" were both nearing the age of fifty.

The first was born when Hayward was twenty-three and not more than a year married, still learning the underground trade. He'd sat up all night in the hospital waiting room, smoking cigarettes and looking to the swinging doors that led to the wards. Somewhere back there, Etta was in labour. More than that he wasn't told.

Near nine the next morning he was led back to the room where she lay exhausted and teary, exhilarated in an other-worldly way that made him feel like a child witnessing naked adult emotion for the first time. He waited at the bedside until she dropped asleep, then asked to be taken to the nursery. He stood outside the large window while a nurse held his son in her arms on the other side of the glass. Tiny fists. Head spi-ralling on the spine, mouth open, as if the child was trying to get free of a bad dream. The nurse's name was Maggie Dawe. She nodded to Hayward after a minute and set the infant back in its crib.

He went to the Imperial for more cigarettes after leaving the hospital, then drove out the back roads to the dam where he parked near the water. He sat there two hours then, lighting each smoke off the butt of the last. Coins of sunlight in motion on the water's dark conveyer belt, his hands shaking as he brought the cigarette to his mouth. The eyelids of his infant boy so translucent he'd thought he could see the colour of the eyes beneath them. He felt transported and desperate some-how, as full of secret submarine life as the lake. The thought of becoming a father hadn't occupied him much in the months leading up to this moment and he was unprepared to feel it as something so implacably permanent, so irrevocable. A lump in his throat, so he could just inhale the smoke, those first hours when he experienced the love of his son only as a grinding, inexorable terror moving through him.

Sitting in the doctor's office that November afternoon as the X-rays and scans went up on the light board, something related to that old fear came back to him, the taste of it in his mouth. The specialist was a small, fastidious man from New Delhi whose silver hair in contrast to the darkness of his skin seemed to cast light, as if it was connected to a battery. He and Hayward had difficulty with each other's accents and Etta was called upon to act as an interpreter.

"He said taking the lung out may not help," she told Hayward, "but it's the only chance you have."

Edgeless spots of darkness, like potato rot, blighting the phosphorescence of healthy tissue.

"And no more cigarettes," she added quietly.

"Bit late for that I expect," Hayward said. He was thinking of the boys, of having to tell them. For the first time in years both sons were coming home for the holidays with their families, Warrick flying down from Labrador City where he worked the open-pit iron ore mines, Glen coming all the way from Alberta.

He said, "It'll have to wait till after Christmas."

"Hayward," Etta said.

He looked across at the doctor. "I can still have a scatter snort if I wants one, can I?" he asked.

The doctor shrugged helplessly and turned to Etta.

"Can he have a drink now and then, he wants to know."

The doctor shrugged again. "Drinks are not being the problem, Mr Hayward. The lung is the problem. There is removing," he said. He pointed up at the series of images, the diffuse glow of them like light through stained glass. "And then there is hoping for the best."

Hayward nodded. "After Christmas," he said.

When he made his way back downstairs, Etta was at the tree. It was weighted down with lights, garlands, a cascade of tinsel. She held half-a-dozen construction paper ornaments made by the boys in grade school. She'd preserved them for decades, and was placing them carefully on the branches. They had called from the airport in Gander an hour before. They were driving rented cars the rest of the way home. Hayward thought of them on the road, two men travelling the empty Black Rock highway, pushing for the place they'd first come to the light. Snow and dark waves of spruce crowding the pavement.

Warrick was only eighteen months old when Etta discovered she was pregnant a second time. The house they were living in was a company duplex heated by a wood stove in the kitchen. Behind cupboards and in closets there was sometimes half an inch of daylight showing where the walls failed to meet the floor. The baby slept with them for warmth, and on the coldest nights of the winter when they woke to him crying to be fed, Hayward went out to stoke the fire, to run water in the bathroom and kitchen to keep the pipes from freezing solid. He remembers coming back to lie beside the child and his wife, the silky hair at the crown of the baby's head tucked close under his chin, the heat between them like something generated purely by emotion. He told Etta it seemed unfair to have more children, that he couldn't imagine loving another the way he did the first.

Etta clucked her tongue. "You have no idea how love works," she said.

He had taken offence to that, thought it was just like a woman to assume a man's incompetence in matters of the heart. Though he simply tipped his head side to side to indicate his disagreement, a motion she couldn't have registered in the dark.

Etta turned from the Christmas tree to look at him standing at the foot of the stairs with his shoes in his hand. He'd begun noticing lately how astonishingly tiny a figure she was, hips invisible under the dress. Frightening to think of the boys inside that body, the fight she must have had to shove them free. The bald wilfulness of it.

She had been right about him of course. He'd had no idea how love works, what he would feel the first time he held Glen in his arms.

"Are you going to put those on?" Etta asked him.

He looked down at the shoes a moment, blinking away the first infuriating sting of tears. "They'll be a while yet getting here," he said.

"I suppose they will." Etta waited with her hands folded in front of her.

There was a new awkwardness between them now, unlike anything they'd known since those first few nights going to bed after they married. A constant sense of something about to be said that kept them on edge.

Hayward said, "Why don't we take a little drive somewhere."

There was nowhere, exactly, to drive to. They skirted the perimeter of the town, moving slowly along streets lined with boarded windows, the desolation interrupted occasionally by houses strung with coloured lights. They drove by the lots where bunkhouses and storehouses and core sheds once stood. It wasn't emptiness they encountered, not even absence. It was loss, an object lesson in the inevitability of grief. The car's engine so quiet they could hear the tires hissing over the frozen pavement.

Hayward turned out the back roads toward the dam, driving parallel for a while with the rail bed, the ties taken up and sold off as firewood when the Company began shipping the ore in trucks during the eighties. The notoriously slow train had been the only way into town before the road went through, endless games of crib and flasks of alcohol circulating among passengers to pass the time. Long nights of drinking that led more than one man into the tiny bathroom, the toilet a seat over a draughty hole in the floor, to vomit onto the tracks passing beneath the car. Enos Hawkins had lost his false teeth that way sometime in the fifties, just shy of town. He walked miles along the rail bed each year he came out moose hunting, his rifle in the crook of his arm, hoping to find those teeth.

"Poor old Enos," Hayward said, as if they had been discussing him aloud.

After they crossed the dam, he parked at the edge of the lake without turning off the engine, headlights shining out over black water. Neither of them spoke. Etta leaned forward to turn on the radio, her face illuminated in the blue light from the dash. Long ropes of static uncoiling as she moved through the dial and then the tinny drone of carols. "The Twelve Days of Christmas."

"I always wondered," Hayward said. "What a pear tree looks like."

Etta shrugged. "Like any tree I guess."

"The pears just hang there, do they? Like apples?"

She smiled out at the water. "Do you remember Wah Lee, Hayward? The one used to do the laundry for the bunkhouse crowd?"

He turned towards her, puzzled.

"Wah Lee had wild cherry trees around his place. Along Bennett's Hill. I used to go down there to pick them when I was a girl. He'd come outside and pull the branches down so I could reach the cherries." She looked into her lap a moment and then back out at the water. "He wasn't as queer as people say he was. He used to have me in for tea after I'd filled my pockets with cherries. Before his wife came over from China. Whatever became of him, I wonder?"

Hayward shook his head. "No idea," he said quietly. It surprised him that there was something about her he didn't know after all this time, even something as odd and inconsequential as this. "I came out here after Warrick was born," he said to her then. "When I left the hospital that morning."

"Out here?" she said.

He nodded his head. "Holly Jolly Christmas" started up on the radio. He shrugged his shoulders helplessly.

Etta waited a long time for him to go on. Then she said, "We should probably be getting back."

Hayward nodded again, relieved. "Alright," he said. But when they reached the paved road at the edge of town he turned away from the house, driving the deserted street toward what had once been Company property.

He had never said a word to anyone about his time smoking cigarettes in the car at the dam after seeing his son for the first time, when he tried to hold down that inexplicable sense of panic. He could hardly credit the fact that he'd brought it up now and had no idea what possessed him to mention it.

It was close to noon, the sun high, when the girl came across the dam in a white blouse and dark skirt. She was still school age and couldn't have been more than sixteen, he knew. He waved to her through the open window and she walked slowly over to the car.

"What are you doing out this way?" he asked her.

She leaned on the window frame and shrugged. "Just walking," she said.

"That's a long ways to just be walking."

She shrugged again, in a way that was both helpless and defiant. There was a sullenness about her that seemed new to him, something she was trying to pass off as maturity. As if being openly dissatisfied with her life was a mark of adulthood.

He motioned with his head. "I can drop you back to town if you like."

They knew each other only in passing. She was the daughter of Cecil Quinlin who worked in the mill and Hayward sometimes saw them together at the Imperial or during events at the Legion. She was a pretty girl and he joined Cecil in teasing her about boyfriends or her precociously developing bustline. He had never thought of her as anything much more than a child. In the car she sat with her back against the door so she faced him, one leg up on the seat. "Can I have a cigarette?" she asked him.

He turned his head away from her, from the sight of the bare skin of her thighs, and stared out at the water. A moment ago he'd been relieved to see her, as if talking to someone might ease his anxiety. But he could feel the uneasiness and fear turning in him now, moving lower in the pit of his stomach, becoming something else altogether. It seemed suddenly illicit to him to be sitting out beyond town limits with this girl. "You're too young to be smoking, aren't you?" he said.

She leaned forward to push the lighter in, then picked out the longest butt she could find in the ashtray and carefully straightened the crushed end. She had fine dark hair that blew about her face in the breeze through the open windows. When the lighter popped, she lit the butt and blew a long line of smoke across the seat. She slipped her shoes off and sat back, putting one foot up on the dashboard. She said, "What else do you think I'm too young for?"

He would have thought she was simply teasing him, a kind of retaliation for the innocent ribbing he'd subjected her to, if there wasn't such an off-hand recklessness to her tone, her posture. If he wasn't feeling a profound recklessness of his own. She was wearing red nail polish, the sleeves of her blouse rolled to her elbows. It occurred to him he had no real idea who she was.

Etta said, "Where are we going now, Hayward?" There was a note of impatience in his wife's voice, but he didn't answer her. The car rumbled over the speed bumps at the border of company property, which was unlit and eerily still, like a graveyard of shipwrecks. Headlights picking out details of ruined machinery, old warehouses on the verge of collapse. On a bare concrete foundation, two ball mills, like the works of some massive timepiece, were slowly going to rust in the open air. Hayward drove past them towards a long, low machine shop that for a time after the mine closed had been a cottage factory producing granite headstones and knick-knacks, slate clocks cut in the shape of the island of Newfoundland.

It had been so long since he thought of his time with the girl that he was surprised to recall so clearly now the urge he had to touch her, knowing he could if he chose to, even if he was wrong to think that was what she wanted. He had turned his head toward her with his mind made up, drunk on the simplicity of it. How quickly he'd be displaced, how the shape of his life would change. Like dropping a bottle onto concrete.

Hayward pulled the car to a stop in front of a high wire fence at the back of the machine shop. It circled a yard of broken stone half buried in snow, rows of monuments tipped on their sides, only the polished corners visible. He reached out to turn off the Christmas carols and pointed towards the far corner where the Virgin Mary stood facing them, her hands turned out toward the headlights.

Etta looked across at him. "Why is she out here?" she asked.

He said, "They couldn't find anyone to take her when the school came down, I expect."

The girl had slipped her shoes off after lighting her cigarette and he turned back to her with his mind made up. He was about to say her name. Angela? Anita? He couldn't remember now. She was wearing dark socks and he saw that the heel on the dash had a hole worn through, showing a quarter-sized circle of flesh. It seemed a hopelessly childish thing, that rent in the cotton fabric. Something unintentionally, almost comically, innocent. He leaned forward to touch his finger gently to the exposed skin. "You've got a hole there, my love," he said.

It was his paternal tone that embarrassed her. She dropped her foot to the floor quickly, pushing her shoes on. "Jesus," the girl said. She turned away to stare out the window, then douted the cigarette butt in the ashtray. She sat fidgeting another minute, her face flushing a deeper and deeper red, and then she said, "I have to go." She wouldn't look at him.

"Alright then," he said. He sat there after she pushed out the door, watching her walk back the way she came, her arms folded tightly across her breasts as if she caught a chill.

He'd come that close to throwing everything away, before he and Etta had hardly made a start. He reached his hand across the seat to find hers in the dark. He said, "Everything that matters to me in this world came through you."

She squeezed his hand in her lap, but didn't look at him. "You're going to have to say something to the boys when they get here," she said. And he knew she was right about that as well.

They sat a long time in silence then, staring at the figure on the opposite side of the yard. The elaborate folds of stone cloth about her head and shoulders in the steady beam of the headlights looked cold, comfortless.

"I keep thinking she must be lonely out here by herself," Hayward said finally. "All Christmas like this."

A light snow had begun falling and the flakes sparked around the statue in the wind before he put the car in reverse and pulled away.

THAT FALL

They followed the hearse in through the country from St. John's, four hours on the Trans-Canada to Notre Dame Junction, the weather cold but surprisingly fine for mid-December, the roads clear. At the Junction they turned north off the main highway, driving on to Twillingate where Grace's mother was to be buried the following morning.

At the funeral home, the driver of the hearse walked with them across the crushed-stone parking lot to the door. She was a young woman just out of mortician's college, no more than twenty-three. She wore black slacks and a short black blazer with the cuffs turned up at the wrists.

Grace said, "Was Mom any trouble on the drive?" and the girl smiled. She had small, perfect teeth. "No, my love," she said. "She was good as gold."

When she disappeared into an office down the hall, Ed said, "She seems happier than someone in her job has a right to be."

"She's just a youngster," Grace told him.

Ed leaned toward Grace's son Isaac, who had flown in from Houston for the funeral. "She'll never have to worry about being out of work anyway," he said.

There was a viewing that evening from seven to nine, Grace's mother laid out in a purple dress that had to be taken in four sizes to fit her wasted body. It had been weeks since Grace saw the old woman wearing her false teeth and her mouth looked too rigid and severe to be real.

Afterwards they stopped at the Anchor Inn Motel and sat downstairs in the nearly empty bar. There was a giant screen on the near wall, a hockey game on with the sound turned down. The players seemed to be moving in slow motion, the game drained of urgency by the silence. Grace wanted a cigarette but was too embarrassed to light up in front of Isaac.

A slender waitress with thickly curled hair to her shoulders brought a tray of drinks to their table and went back to her book behind the bar. Ed thought she was the woman they'd seen recently in a news report, a follow-up story on a national survey in which Newfoundlanders claimed to have sex more frequently than anyone else in Canada. There was a clip of a slender woman with thickly curled hair playing darts in this very bar, saying mainlanders were too uptight to have sex as often as was natural. "Take me now," she'd said. She pointed the shaft of a dart at the interviewer. She spoke with the intensity of someone who is often disbelieved. "I won't get home tonight till two and I (pause) will still (pause) have sex."

Grace said no, the woman on the news was taller than this one.

Ed took a long drag on his cigarette. "Everyone looks taller on television," he said.

They stayed to the end of the second period and then drove to the old house that had been sitting empty since Grace's mother came to live with her in St. John's that August. The neighbours had turned on the heat and left lights on for them and put out a Saran-wrapped plate of tea buns and cheese in the kitchen. Grace and Ed went up to bed while Isaac watched the end of the game on the tiny black-and-white in the living room. Grace could hear the murmur of it from downstairs, the sound of skates creasing ice, the rise and fall of crowd noise. She turned to Ed and moved over him, pushing her face into the skin of his neck to muffle the rise and fall of her own voice.

Her mother had lived alone in the family home for three decades after Grace left to do her nurses' training at the Salvation Army hospital in St. John's. She had a rotary dial telephone, an oil stove, a black-and-white television that brought in three snowy channels. She grew her own potatoes and cabbage, gave herself insulin injections morning and evening. Never forgot a birthday or anniversary. "Good as a quartz watch," Grace used to say. "She never needs winding."

It was a neighbour of her mother's who called late that summer. She'd noticed that the lights stayed out in the house as it grew dark. When she stepped across the road, she found Grace's mother on the chesterfield where she'd been lying for hours, incoherent and unresponsive. A week later Grace drove out from St. John's to get her.

The old home always seemed like a doll's house when she came back to it, the ceilings so low Grace could place her palms flat against them, the stairs so narrow a suitcase had to be carried ahead or behind you. The kitchen just large enough for a small table, the narrow daybed tucked along one wall behind the stove where Grace had convalesced the summer she turned seven.

There was a spate of unusually hot weather near the end of May that year, a week of stifling humidity that made the nights almost as unbearable as the days. Grace's mother dragged the bathing tub into the yard and filled it with water from the well. The well water was so frigid that Grace had to wait a full day for the temperature to rise and even then could stand the chill only so long, getting out of the tub periodically to warm herself in the intense heat of the sun when her bones began to ache. She spent hours see-sawing between those extremes and that night came down with a fever that soaked her bedsheets. In the morning her mother discovered blood in her chamber pot.

At the time Grace's father was spending eleven months of the year working underground in Black Rock, two days travel by boat and train from their home in Twillingate. After Grace was admitted to hospital, the doctor advised her mother to send for him. It was an infection of the kidney, something serious and unpredictable, and there was no way of knowing for certain if Grace would survive. Her mother nodded as this was explained to her. "I don't have a telephone," she said.

"You can use the hospital phone, of course," the doctor told her.

She called the main office in Black Rock, explaining herself to a secretary who patched her through to an office where a man's voice came on the line. "Mrs. Lane," the voice said. "I'm sorry, we've been trying to reach you."

By the time Grace was released from hospital her father's body had been transported home and buried. She had a notion of how she was expected to react to the news of his death, but in the three years he had worked in Black Rock he'd become mostly a stranger and it seemed barely to touch her. She was still recovering from her illness besides, and the details of the world around her felt muffled and foreign, drained somehow of their normal heft. She felt as if her father had simply moved to another job farther afield which meant only that she would see him less. It hardly seemed a loss at all. The way her mother spoke of it suggested as much, her tone one of tired acceptance. She sat on a chair beside the daybed to explain how he had died in an underground accident, falling between the car and the loading dock at the end of his shift. She answered Grace's questions as if reporting an incident from the newspaper, without betraying any sign of grief or anger or bewilderment. It never occurred to Grace at the time how hard-won that calm would have been. It wasn't until after she'd become a mother herself that she realized it was likely there for her benefit alone.

She considered this as she collected her mother's bags from the bedroom and carried them awkwardly downstairs, then out to the car. The forecast called for freezing rain in the afternoon and she could feel the threat of it in the wind. When she came back inside she found her mother staring out the single tiny window in the kitchen, the landwash falling away to the grey ocean beyond it.

"We should go," Grace told her. Calling up the calm within her, willing it into her voice.

"Hold on," her mother said. She was wearing a long grey raglan and black shoes, the strap of her handbag looped over the crook of her elbow. She said, "I'll never look out that window again." There was an odd note in her mother's voice, in the way she said "that window." As if it wasn't her but the window that was about to be taken away from the house for good.

The tests showed her mother's kidneys were deteriorating, a complication related to her diabetes. She went for dialysis three afternoons a week at the Health Sciences Centre, but it was clear there was no hope of recovery and the sessions left the old woman feeling exhausted and numb. It took two days to get up and around properly afterwards. She said it was like being struck by lightning.

"You've been struck by lightning, have you?" Grace said.

Her mother was sitting with her hand over her mouth and nose. She looked away out the living room window. "You know what I mean," she said.

After the third week she refused further treatment and through that fall her body slowly poisoned itself. She moved about the house with a cane, then with a walker. Eventually she needed help to shower, to go to the bathroom, then simply to feed herself. When the length of the hallway became unmanageable, Grace took a leave of absence from her nursing job. She moved the La-Z-Boy into her mother's room and fed her cups of soup, Jell-O and ice-cream, bread soaked in mugs of milky tea.

Her mother began losing her bearings, often living at the old house in Twillingate in her head. At first, there was a childish certainty to her confusion that was almost comical. She mistook Grace for an aunt, for her mother, a friend she hadn't seen since she was a girl. "Where are you now, my love?" Grace would ask her.

"Sure, I'm at Annie's."

"Annie Reid's house, is it? In Crow Head?"

"*Yes*, in Crow Head."

Annie dead, her house torn down and replaced by a hardware store in the 1950s. Grace laughed to disguise the surge of helplessness that buckled through her. Her mother stared, indignant. Try as she might, she couldn't see the humour in being at Annie Reid's house in Crow Head or understand why she was being teased about it. "Where are *you*?" she'd ask.

Consternation was the word that came to Grace's mind, watching her mother struggle, the old woman's childhood crowding in on her mind like weeds choking out a garden. Near the end she was sometimes lucid and lost simultaneously. One afternoon she turned to Grace and said, "You know, Gracie is the only one I got left."

She nodded her head. "Grace told me how much she loves you," she said.

Her mother's room was just large enough for her single bed and the La-Z-Boy chair and the commode Grace signed out on loan from the Red Cross. The air was close with the smell of bedsore liniment and the diapers her mother was reduced to wearing, and Grace would open the window for the breeze, despite the cold. In heavy weather, when the wind was right, the sound of the foghorn carried up from the shoreline two miles east. If her mother was lucid enough to register it, she made a face and turned her head away. "Oh my," she'd say. "Close that window would you?"

"Why, what's wrong with a bit of fresh air?"

"I hates the sound of that fog horn."

Her mother had lived in the lee of that wail all her life and it made Grace feel suddenly afraid and somehow saddened to learn how much she disliked it. It added to the panic she had begun to feel about herself. For the first time in years she dreaded going to bed alone, lay awake for hours on one side of the mattress, staring into the darkness. Her new loneliness something with presence and heft, a physical thing chafing at her insides. She was sure it would show up on a chest X-ray like a tumour, a cloudy mass with clearly defined edges.

Grace's friends could see the change in her, but they mistook it for something simpler than it was, for fatigue or sadness. She needed time away from the house, they told her. When she insisted she was fine they nodded their heads quickly and looked down at their shoes, trying to hide their frustration with what they referred to among themselves as Grace's advanced state of denial.

Two of the younger nurses she worked with at Emergency came for her unannounced one Friday night. They'd made their own arrangements to have a home-care nurse stay with her mother, and they stood in the doorway with their coats and shoes on, telling Grace how much better she'd feel if she would only relax for an evening. Grace was surprised at the strength of her reluctance, at the measure of guilt she felt when she walked out to the waiting taxi in a dress and high-heeled shoes. It was unlike anything she'd experienced since telling Isaac she was divorcing his father.

The nurses took her to a small martini bar on Duckworth Street that featured black lights around the baseboards, a relentlessly nebulous soundtrack of acid jazz and trip-hop and house music. Grace had never tried a martini before and couldn't finish it, the mix of gin and vermouth too unadulterated. She went up to the bar to ask for help picking something else from the elaborate drink menu. Ed wore a dark vest over a white shirt that had the hue of purple neon in the black light. He suggested something called a Stinger. "Good for what ails you," he said brightly.

Grace glanced up at him. Younger than she was, she decided, mid-forties or so. Just past the age when he might be considered good-looking, but not so far that he'd lost the ease that his good looks had conferred. Not predatory, she could see. A cocky, professional flirt. She turned back to the drink list, furious with herself for agreeing to come here. "My mother's dying," she said without looking up. She expected it would shut the man up, wipe the smirk off his face.

He gave her a Stinger on the house. "Lost Mom last year," he told her quietly.

She raised the glass. "Will this help?"

"Briefly," he said. He smiled at her. Then he said, "Not much, no."

Grace left with the other nurses an hour-and-a-half later, then came back to the bar alone. She'd had three Stingers by then and ordered another. After the bar closed up she and Ed took a cab to Signal Hill, stepping out into the empty parking lot near the Cabot Tower. The stone tower was floodlit with stark white light, as if the building was being subjected to some relentless interrogation. There was a low wall around the parking lot that they sat against and they stared out over St. John's. Streetlights terraced the hills above the harbour, clustered rows undulating miles back into the country, a sprawling grid of energy. It was near three in the morning. They could see the cab descending the unlit road below them, taillights swinging lazily through the winding turns. The red glow flared brighter when the brakes were applied, like someone taking a drag on a cigarette in the dark.

Ed said, "We should have asked him to wait."

Grace looked across at him. He had thinning red hair. His

mouth turned down on one side even when he smiled, which gave him an air of tired honesty. She shrugged. "I could use the walk," she told him.

Ed nodded and took a pack of cigarettes out of an inside pocket of his coat.

Grace had quit cold turkey when she was thirty-four, the same year she divorced Isaac's father. She had a pack-a-day habit through her marriage, although there was only one cigarette in a dozen that she really enjoyed. Sex with Isaac's father had been much the same and it had been years since she craved either one.

Ed gave her a wary look when she reached out and helped herself, fishing a cigarette from its neat row. He said, "I didn't see you smoking at the bar."

"It's not a regular thing with me," she told him.

Ed cupped his hands to light her cigarette, then his own. Grace walked across to the opposite side of the parking lot where the hills dipped and rose and then fell away toward the ocean. She could hear the surf breaking on the headlands off in the distance and she leaned over the wall as far as she could, staring into the dark as if her eyes might adjust eventually, find enough light to make out shapes in the blackness. She could feel the pulse of the city lights at her back, the nicotine buzz of electricity coursing through thousands of miles of wire and cable. And the dark ocean rolling hundreds of feet beyond her blind stare. It was the beginning of October. She had no idea what she was doing here with this man.

"Maybe we should head home out of it," Ed shouted from across the flat expanse of pavement.

She had never slept with a stranger before and was

prepared to be profoundly disappointed. She never expected to hear from him again.

After her divorce, Grace made a conscious effort at *self-improvement,* as if the failure of her marriage was a sign of some personal shortcoming she could fix by giving up smoking or joining Weight Watchers. She experimented with yoga and transcendental meditation, enrolled in several night courses at the university. She managed to stay off the cigarettes for Isaac's sake, but abandoned the diet after week seven. She'd lost nine-and-a-half pounds, but her nails were chewed to the quick.

As for Sociology and Psychology, she'd dealt with it all a hundred times on the hospital wards, and there was nothing much new or interesting in any of her courses. She stopped taking notes, doodling aimlessly instead, or revising a long list of household repairs she couldn't afford. She often forgot which class she was sitting through and looked up from her list one evening in Anatomy, surprised to see a diagram of the female genitals on the overhead screen. The professor was in his mid-thirties, with a goatee and a prominent bald spot. He held a metal pointer that extended and retracted like a TV antennae, and he was circling a small area of the diagram repeatedly with the plastic tip. Grace had been working as a nurse for fifteen years at the time. She had been married nearly as long.

She went to Isaac's room as soon as she got home. He was in Grade 8 that year and she looked through a stack of books and scribblers until she found the material from his Sex Education class. She flipped through photo-copied essays and questionnaires and diagrams until she found it there. A simple sketch, a line connecting the tiny nub of nerve endings to the unfamiliar italicized word. There was a note beneath it in Isaac's hand-writing: *The clitoris contains twice the number of nerve endings located in the penis.* She sat staring, her arms folded under her breasts, not quite believing her body could have kept such a secret from her. That her thirteen-year-old son could know more about her body than she did herself.

The old house in Twillingate was one of the last on the island to have indoor plumbing installed. When Grace was a girl there was a cast-iron wood stove in the kitchen. One night a week she sat in a wooden tub in front of the fire and after she went to bed she would hear her mother using the same water: the wet slap of the facecloth, the cupfuls lifted and sluiced across her back.

While her mother was still able to get around that fall, Grace helped her negotiate her way into the tub on Wednesdays and Saturdays. She used the hand-held showerhead while her mother sat on a plastic stool, her arms folded across her stomach like a woman waiting at a bus stop. She was seventy-seven years old. Grace had never before seen her naked.

During the last month of her mother's life, Grace bathed her in her bed, rolling her gently from one side to the other to wash her back and buttocks and legs, her wattled neck and arms, the breasts she had nursed at. The tuft of beautiful silver pubic hair.

Three nights that fall, Grace was convinced her mother was hours from dying, her breath shallow and clotted with fluid, her left hand flailing helplessly against her chest. Grace called Ed to come keep her company after his shift at the bar and they sat up together through the small hours of the morning, taking turns at the open window, blowing smoke into the darkness. After sunrise her mother would come to herself, exhausted but remarkably lucid, like a woman who has just endured a difficult labour.

During the first week of November Grace's mother began asking, "Is it my birthday yet?"

No one had expected she would live this long.

"Ten more sleeps," Grace told her. As if her mother was a child anticipating Christmas. "Eight more sleeps."

By this time Ed was at the house every day, helping Grace lift her mother from her bed to the chair, from the chair to the commode. Her mother took him for another of the nameless home-care nurses who came and went. At some point during each visit, he and Grace made love while her mother drifted in and out of sleep in her room. Grace's appetite surprised and embarrassed her. She had never been so greedy for pleasure and it felt like a betrayal of some kind. But the shame she felt simply made the craving more intense, more compelling.

The day before her mother's birthday, when Grace saw in the old woman's face some sign that she was present and alert, she said, "I've been wanting to tell you Mom. I've met someone."

The watery blue eyes searching her face.

"I've met a man."

Her mother made a motion with her head, as if she was acknowledging an acquaintance on the street. "Proper thing," she said.

Grace smiled at her. As far as she knew, her mother hadn't been with anyone after the death of her husband forty years earlier. She didn't know how much that was a conscious choice and how much simply circumstance. She said, "Were you happy, Mom?"

Her mother stared, her eyes shifting quickly back and forth. It was clear she didn't understand what was being asked of her. "I was happy to have you," she said.

The next day Grace and Ed sat on the edge of the bed and sang "Happy Birthday" to her mother in her chair. A cake in the old woman's lap held two candles, to mark her age—78— each number with a shifting cap of flame. Ed took a picture of Grace kneeling beside her mother to help blow out the candles. She managed to speak lucidly to several people on the phone, asking Isaac about his newborn baby daughter. "She's American, that one," her mother said.

In the weeks following the small birthday celebration, Grace's mother never again got up from her bed. Lying beside Ed in the afternoons, after they'd made love, Grace tried to put herself in her mother's position. She would watch the ceiling and imagine it was the last tiny landscape she would ever look upon. That she would never walk from this room with its mauve walls and chocolate-coloured carpet, or sit up on her own again, or eat a proper meal. She managed to stir up a peculiar sense of claustrophobia in herself, but it felt contrived and weightless, like the fear evoked by a carnival ride.

Ed moved closer to her, waking from a brief sleep, his

cock hardening against her thigh as they shifted their bodies towards one another. She reached down to touch him, to feel the pulse and heat of the man centred there. This was real to her. What was happening in the room across the hall was a long, shapeless bad dream she would eventually wake from, though her mother would not. And in that sense, she knew, it was something the old woman had to suffer alone.

Ed leaned his face into her neck and reached up to wipe the tears from her face with the palm of his hand. "Gracie," he said. "Grace."

"I'm alright," she said. "I'm okay."

She turned to kiss him, the bitter salt taste passed back and forth between them, and she moved slowly down his body then to take his cock into her mouth. Ed gathered her hair at the back of her head, holding it tight in his fist while she sucked him, and she felt the sting of it all the way to her toes.

Her mother died just before light, a month to the day after her birthday. They were changing the sheet beneath her after another nightlong vigil, Ed standing against the wall and leaning over the old woman to roll her onto her side, Grace lifting the sheet away from the opposite corners.

"Gracie, she's throwing up," he said.

She looked over her mother's shoulder, at the black bile dribbling from her mouth. "She's gone," Grace said.

Ed looked up quickly. "What?"

Grace was shaking her head slowly. "She's gone," she whispered.

Ed eased the woman's body onto her back and they both

stood at the bedside, staring at her. Grace held her hand to her mouth a moment and then weighted her mother's eyelids closed with her fingers.

"I don't know what she was holding on so long for, poor soul," Ed said.

Grace brought a pan of warm water to the bedside to wipe her face and neck, to wash the emaciated limbs. She wanted her mother's body touched with love one last time before the hearse arrived to collect her.

Ed leaned over her, one hand on Grace's back, the other touching her mother's grey hair, her forehead. "She's so hot," he said, surprised.

Grace opened her mouth but couldn't force a word past the knot galling her throat.

It was the body's internal organs, the heat of them exiting through the skin, dissipating in the cool air of the sick room.

The forecast called for snow the day of the funeral, but all morning a cold, steady drizzle of rain came down. The open water beyond the coves, the low hills of meadow grass and bedrock lost to December fog.

The funeral procession drove up a long dirt road into spruce woods. The hearse passed through rows of headstones to the back of the cemetery. When her father was buried here forty years earlier the grave had to be blasted with dynamite. Along the fence Grace could see the front-end loader that was used to jackhammer her mother's grave out of the rock beside her father's plot.

Ed stood to one side of her, Isaac to the other, holding an

umbrella. Those old hard words from the minister as the casket settled down.

One morning shortly before she died, bedridden, unable to turn herself or move her legs, unsure who her daughter was or how old she might be or where she was lying, her mother had looked at Grace and said, "I'm getting up now the once."

"Yes, my love," Grace said. It was no use to argue, she knew. They stared at one another a moment longer and then her mother turned her head toward the wall.

Ed touched Grace's elbow through her coat. The mourners were moving away from the grave to get in out of the weather. "We should go, Grace," he said.

The sound of the foghorn pressed in over the trees and subsided like the tide.

"Grace," he said again.

She nodded her head but didn't move from the spot where she stood.

"Hold on," she said.

ACKNOWLEDGEMENTS

Everyone's a critic. I'm grateful to the following in particular: Joy Gugeler, Helen Humphreys, Martha Kanya-Forstner, Wanda Mattson, Janice McAlpine, Amber McCart, Lisa Moore, Alison Pick, Carolyn Smart, Julie van der Meulen, and Megan Williams.

Many people fed these stories by sharing some of their own. I'd like to thank my parents, Al Lear, Johnny Fitzgerald, Moody and Olive Starks, Jim Merrigan, and Eli Reid, for their (sometimes unwitting) generosity.

Thanks to the editors who have published some of these stories previously—
"After Image" in *The Malahat Review*.
"Break & Enter" in *Blood & Aphorisms*.
"Celestials" in *Prism international*.
"Praxis" in *The Fiddlehead*.
"Diaspora" in *Prairie Fire*.
"Miracles" in *TickleAce*.
"Roots" in *The New Quarterly* and in *STORY* (US)
"Serendipity" in *TickleAce*, *The Journey Prize Anthology*, and *Dreaming Home* (Paperplates Books).

"Skin" in *Dandelion*.

"That Fall" was commissioned for and broadcast on CBC Radio's Festival of Fiction, later published in *The New Quarterly* and in the anthology *Victory Meat* (Anchor Canada).

"What Possessed Him" in *The Globe and Mail*.